W9-BFU-650

A MARRIAGE OF
INCONVENIENCE

Recent Titles by Marion Chesney from Severn House

THE EDUCATION OF MISS PATTERSON
THE GHOST AND LADY ALICE
LADY ANNE'S DECEPTION
LADY LUCY'S LOVER
THE VISCOUNT'S REVENGE

A MARRIAGE OF INCONVENIENCE

Marion Chesney

SEVERN
SH
HOUSE

This title first published in Great Britain 1997 by
SEVERN HOUSE PUBLISHERS LTD of
9–15 High Street, Sutton, Surrey SM1 1DF.
First published in hardcover format in the USA 1997 by
SEVERN HOUSE PUBLISHERS INC. of
595 Madison Avenue, New York, NY 10022.

British Library Cataloguing in Publication Data

Chesney, Marion
    A marriage of inconvenience
    1. English fiction – 20th century
    I. Title
    823.9'14 [F]

    ISBN 0-7278-5121-7

Typeset by Palimpsest Book Production Limited,
Polmont, Stirlingshire, Scotland.
Printed and bound in Great Britain by
Hartnolls Ltd, Bodmin, Cornwall.

Chapter One

Mrs. Chadbury was wondering whether she ought to go into a decline. She felt she could not cope with her daughter, Isabella, any longer.

Another London Season had just drawn to its weary close; another round of turtle dinners, subscription balls at Almack's assembly rooms, plays and operas and concerts. And Isabella was still unwed. Mrs. Chadbury, seated at her toilet table, studied her reflection in the glass. She decided she looked unfashionably healthy, from her plump figure to her rosy cheeks and her shining brown hair, which held not a trace of gray. No one would believe her if she said she was going into a decline.

But, oh, to escape from responsibility for Isabella!

The wretched girl had been the belle of this Season as much as she had of the last. She was possessed of a beautiful face and a handsome dowry. Suitors had come in droves, and Isabella had turned them all down flat, in a finicky way, as if turning down bonnets that she thought would not suit her. This one was too showy, that one too boring, the other too loud.

Isabella, reflected Mrs. Chadbury, was thoroughly spoiled. But how could either she or her husband have guessed the damage they were doing when they indulged her every whim? For she had hitherto been sweet natured and kind. She had been born to Mrs. Chadbury after that lady had suffered a series of unfortunate miscarriages. To be blessed with such an exquisite, such a beautiful daughter had seemed to them like a gift from the gods. They were very rich and so could give her the best of everything; the best jewels to sparkle at her throat and in her hair, the finest silks to adorn her perfect figure.

The trouble had started at the first Season and had carried on into the second. She had become, almost instantly, wantonly flirtatious, encouraging suitors only to send them away.

From being the envy of other society matrons, Mrs. Chadbury knew she had become an object of pity.

The door opened and her husband, Mr. Charles Chadbury, walked in. He was a tall, thin man, elegantly dressed, with white hair cropped in the latest Brutus cut. He was not handsome, nor had he ever been, but he had kind eyes and a diffident manner, both of which had won Mrs. Chadbury's heart all those years ago.

"We have a problem, Mrs. Chadbury," he said, sitting down in an upright chair next to her.

"Isabella *again*?" asked his wife faintly. "What has she done?"

"It is not what she has done. Rather it is what she is about to do. Lord Rupert Fitzjohn is calling this afternoon, having gained my permission to pay his addresses to Isabella."

"Lord Rupert?" Mrs. Chadbury wrenched her memory. "Of course," she said, her face clearing. "Very suitable. Handsome, rich, young . . . about twenty-three, is he not?"

"When did suitability count with Isabella?" Her husband sighed. "I have told Isabella to put on one of her best gowns and make herself ready. To which she said, as usual, 'Yes, Papa.' I asked her if she would entertain his suit, to which she said, as usual, 'I will consider the matter very carefully, Papa.' "

Mrs. Chadbury dabbed some rice powder on her nose and said wistfully, "If only she would accept him. Perhaps she is simply being flighty because of her youth."

"Youth? She is *nineteen*, Mrs. Chadbury. A grown woman and shortly to be an old maid, an ape leader, if she continues so."

"We shall be leaving for the country on the morrow," said his wife, "and we will both feel better when we have shaken the dust of London from our heels. I shall talk to Isabella . . . again. Mayhap this time I can talk some sense into her pretty head." She rang the bell and ordered a servant to tell Miss Isabella to attend her mother.

Mr. Chadbury rose and deposited a kiss on his wife's cheek. "I will leave you alone with her," he said.

Isabella entered her mother's boudoir shortly after her father had left. She was indeed extraordinarily beautiful. She had thick, chestnut hair with

3

a natural curl, a clear skin, a short straight nose, and large hazel eyes fringed with thick black lashes. All her movements were graceful. She was wearing a high-waisted morning gown of white muslin ornamented with a pink sprig.

"I am come in answer to your summons," said Isabella. "You are no doubt going to lecture me on the merits of Lord Rupert Fitzjohn."

"No, I am going to remind you again of your duty to your parents," said Mrs. Chadbury. "We have endured two Seasons in London on your behalf, only to see you break hearts and remain unwed. You will give Lord Rupert's offer your full consideration. You cannot be looking for love in marriage as, so far, you seem to be incapable of that emotion. It is time you thought of setting up your own household and having your own nursery."

"Yes, Mama. Believe me, I will really think very hard about Lord Rupert's offer."

"Do that. If you reject him, then when we return to Cornwall, your father and I must begin to think very seriously of arranging a marriage for you."

Isabella gave a rippling laugh. "You would not do that. Never fear, Mama, Lord Rupert will find me the soul of courtesy."

Lord Rupert Fitzjohn strolled into Malmbrooke Square in London's fashionable West End and approached the Chadburys' town house. He was a tall young man with thick brown hair, a tanned face, fine black eyes, and full sensual lips. His waist was a trifle too thick to please sticklers for high fashion,

as were his ankles, but his shoulders were broad
and his long feet were fashionably narrow.

He had never proposed marriage to any woman
before and, up until he had seen Isabella Chadbury,
had not intended to. Why saddle oneself with one
woman when there were so many delights to be enjoyed in London and for only a little money? The
fact that he had never before gone courting and had
always paid for the delights of the flesh meant that
he had never met with a rebuff and so fancied himself as a veritable Adonis. But now he longed to
make Isabella Chadbury his, to crush all that cool
beauty in his arms, to be an object of envy.

He was not surprised that Mr. Chadbury had
given him permission to court Isabella. Lord Rupert knew his own worth. He was rich and handsome, and he knew he was privately listed as one
of the best catches on the marriage market.

That the Chadburys were extremely rich as well
was a bonus, the icing on the cake.

A correct butler ushered him into the hall of the
Chadburys' town house and took his hat and cane,
murmuring that he would conduct Lord Rupert
straight upstairs to the drawing room.

The faint look of strain on Mr. and Mrs. Chadbury's faces escaped Lord Rupert. He had eyes only
for Isabella. When he entered, she was seated at
the window, the sun shining on her thick chestnut
hair. She had changed into a lilac gown of French
cut that emphasized the perfection of her figure,
the deep neckline displaying the whiteness of her
bosom.

She rose as he entered and curtsied low, mur-

5

muring that yes, indeed, she did remember Lord Rupert and had danced with him the evening before.

After a few courtesies and some brief conversation, Mr. and Mrs. Chadbury withdrew to leave the "happy" couple alone.

Isabella was once more seated. She had been hemming a handkerchief and a workbasket was open at her feet.

"You know why I am come?" he asked.

"Oh, yes, indeed."

Isabella smoothed the unfinished handkerchief into a neat square and put it into her workbasket. As she bent over the workbasket, he stared down the front of her dress, his senses quickening. Well, better get it over with. He was about to go down on one knee when Isabella held up a hand.

"I am entertaining you, my lord," she said, "because my parents told me to, but I fear I must reject your suit."

At first, he was too astonished to be angry.

"Why?"

"Why?" echoed Isabella on a sigh. "I fear I do not wish to become married at present. I have nothing against you, my lord. After all, I do not know you."

Her coolness, her very detachment, began to enrage him. He could hardly believe his ears.

"Do you mean you have the temerity to turn down my offer?"

"That is a harsh way of putting it, my lord, but in a nutshell . . . yes."

Suddenly the anger left his face, and he laughed.

"I know what it is, you sly puss, you are flirting with me. You are going to accept me anyway, so let us not play games."

Her voice was cool and incisive. "I do not play games. I would suggest you do not prolong this distressing interview. I have no intention, my lord, of becoming your wife, either today or at any time in the future, near or far. Good day, my lord." She saw the blazing anger in his eyes and reminded herself quickly that she was in a house full of servants and that her parents were probably outside the door.

"Then hear this, Isabella Chadbury," he said. "No one rejects and insults Lord Rupert Fitzjohn and remains unscathed. One day quite soon, you will be *begging* me to marry you." He bent over her, and she stared up at him, unflinching.

Then he turned on his heel and left the room. Isabella sat very still. Soon she heard the street door slam.

Mr. and Mrs. Chadbury came into the drawing room and surveyed their daughter. Mr. Chadbury was the first to speak.

"So another rejection," he said. "And one too many. Listen to me, Isabella, you will now have a marriage arranged for you, and you will have no say in the matter. Do you understand?"

"Yes, Papa," Isabella said meekly, although she did not believe a word of it. Her parents were too fond, too indulgent.

"Very well, we will say no more about the matter at present."

And neither they did. So Isabella inwardly heaved a sigh of relief. Tomorrow she would be on the way back to beloved Cornwall, to her home, Appleton House. She could resume her favorite pursuits of walking, riding, painting, and sewing, and her parents would soon forget about getting her married off.

She gave a wry little smile. They could not know how she longed to be an old maid.

Once when she was sixteen, she had been full of dreams of love and romance. Although she had been too young to make her come-out, she and her parents had been visiting London to enjoy the plays and operas and were on their way back to Cornwall. They had stopped for the night at a posting house, seeing nothing very much of the other guests at the inn because they had their own suite of rooms that included a private parlor and dining room. Just as they were finishing dinner, the landlord came in to say that a party of young bloods and their women had descended on the posting house, adding significantly that it would be as well if the ladies kept to their quarters.

But when her parents were asleep, Isabella had become curious to have a closer look at these wild guests. She had earlier seen one of them in the courtyard below. He had been a young and dashing-looking man with curly fair hair and bright blue eyes, just the sort of man she often dreamed of.

She had therefore risen and dressed and had made her way along the open gallery outside her room, which overlooked the main courtyard. There was a jolly sound of music coming from the public dining room, and she remembered the landlord saying that the roisterers had taken it over for the evening.

All she wanted to do was to take a look round the door and see if she could see that beautiful young man. Like many sixteen-year-old girls, she enjoyed long romantic dreams. Perhaps *he* might see *her* and ask her to join the festivities.

The passage to the dining room was dark, but the door of the room was wide open, and she saw clearly what was going on within. Shocked and trembling, rooted to the ground, she stood and stared.

Some of the women were stark naked and were dancing wildly with flushed and drunken men. And her beautiful young man? Minus his breeches, he was rutting on the floor with a naked woman while his friends cheered him on. How she at last found the strength to move, she did not know, but she made her way back to her room where she was violently sick.

So that was what men were like. That was what they *did*! But not to her. Never to her. She could not tell her mother about what she had seen. Ladies did not know of such things, did not speak of them, did not even know the words to describe them.

Isabella had been delighted to find herself such a success in London when she had first appeared on the social scene. Naively, she had hoped that that would be enough to please her parents. But the very suggestion that she would not even have the courtesy to speak to the first of her suitors had made her normally mild and indulgent parents very angry indeed. And so Isabella had seen them one after the other, calmly rejecting proposals of marriage. It never crossed her mind that any of her courtiers might be hurt, or offended, or angry. Men did not really suffer from any of the finer feelings when it came to women. They played at it, like a game, sighing and sending flowers and poems. Isabella knew that under the elegant clothes and manners of the Regency beau lurked a slavering satyr. What had poetry and romance to do with what she had witnessed that evening? And the beautiful young man? He had asked her to dance during her first Season, and she had immediately pleaded the headache and asked to be taken home.

The first tremulous awakenings of love and romance had been nipped in the bud by that dreadful party at the posting house. She would never forget it. She would remain cool and chaste and virginal for the rest of her life. She had friends in London of her own age. She had never confided in one of them. Ladies did not speak of such matters in a social world hedged in by euphemisms. Being sick with drink was described as "cascading," and flatulence as "voluntary posterior declamations." Any man in this hard drinking age who suffered from delirium tremens would describe one of his fits casually as the Horrors. The ton abounded with "Don'ts," although there were odd double standards. One did not say "legs" to another lady. That would be impolite. Everyone knew that. And yet Isabella had heard two middle-aged duchesses arguing over which of them had the best legs, ending up with hitching up their skirts for a competition. It was hinted that love could take place outside marriage, but woe betide any married woman who was foolish enough to be found out. A great many ladies of the ton committed adultery, but they would gleefully turn and rend the reputation of one of their more unfortunate sisters who had been discovered by her husband to be conducting an affair. Ladies were expected to be sensitive, delicate creatures, never to be found guilty of any coarseness; yet at a grand dinner party Isabella had attended with her parents, several of the ladies had risen from their seats during the dinner and had gone over to a commode in the corner of the dining room to relieve themselves. Of course one did not comment on it for a lady did not *see* such things.

So Isabella kept the secret of the posting house locked up inside her brain.

All she had to do was to wait until they were all comfortably settled at Appleton House once more and then persuade her parents that there was little point in taking her to London for another Season.

She would have been reassured had she known that her parents had already decided that she had had her last London Season, but she would have been distressed to know the plans for her future.

"We must discuss this affair with our acquaintance. Some young man from the Duchy would be suitable," said Mrs. Chadbury.

"Perhaps not necessarily so young," said Mr. Chadbury. "But I cannot think of anyone at the moment. We'll ask Tremayne."

The Earl and Countess of Tremayne were at that moment seated in the shabby morning room of their

Cornish Tregar Castle. Parts of the cliff outside had begun to crumble into the sea, and yesterday two end rooms in the east wing had disappeared with a great rumble. They had not been important rooms. In fact they had not been in use for some time, but the earl and countess felt it was the beginning of the end. Soon more cliff would crumble, taking more rooms with it. "And then us," said the countess. Although it was breakfast time, she was drinking champagne, which she considered the only thing to restore her shattered nerves. She was a small, dainty woman with hair of an improbable gold. Her husband was a large and shabby creature, rather childlike, who looked out at the world in an occasionally baffled way as if wondering why the good Lord should continue to pile such misery on him. "It's like the plagues of Egypt," he remarked. "Next thing, it'll be raining frogs, mark my words."

"Silly old cliffs," the countess said petulantly. "Why can't they stay where they are? And no money to do anything about it. If we had money, it would not matter if this drafty, miserable place sank to the bottom of the briny deep."

"The what?"

"The *sea*, precious."

"Oh."

"If only Harry were here," the countess went on, "he would know what to do."

Lord Harry was their only son. They had a seventeen-year-old daughter, Lady Lucy, who at that moment had just joined them and was filling a champagne glass for herself, guessing that her parents were too worried about something to notice what she was drinking.

"Don't see what Harry could do about the demned cliffs," remarked the earl. "Stand there like King Canute."

"King Canute ordered the sea to go back," Lucy pointed out. "He didn't do anything about cliffs. Why can't I have a Season?"

"Can't afford it," her mother said. "Maybe next year. Harry wrote and said something about prize money."

Lucy brightened, and then her face fell. "But this dreadful war might go on for a hundred years." She was a plump, cheerful girl, rather slatternly in her dress.

A footman came in and handed a letter to the earl.

He opened it and read it carefully. "The Chadburys are back." he said. "Request the pleasure of our company for dinner."

"Thank goodness for that," said the countess. "They keep a good table. Pity they don't have a son for Lucy. Do they say anything about an engagement for Isabella?"

"No."

"That means she hasn't taken again," said the countess. "All that fortune and beauty. But she's a cold fish, that girl."

"Not with me," said Lucy. "We always have fun." She hiccupped.

"Stop drinking champagne," the countess snapped. "*I* am drinking it for medicinal reasons.

Do you know a part of the east wing went over the cliff last night?"

Lucy brightened. "I must go and look. How do you mean, went over the cliff? You make it sound as if someone had shoved it."

"The cliffs, dear Lucy, crumbled." The countess sighed and raised her small, dainty, slippered feet and rested them on the back of a shabby deerhound that was snoring on the floor. "Look if you must, but don't fall over."

Lucy scampered off, and a footman brought in the morning's post.

"Bills, bills, bills," grumbled the earl, flicking through them. "Oh, here's an interesting one. Could be from Harry." He opened it up and read it quickly. "Listen to this. He's at Portsmouth! He had the fever and was invalided home from the Peninsula, but he said the voyage back did him the world of good and he should be with us shortly, although he thinks he has to stay in Portsmouth for about another ten days."

"Hooray!" cried the countess. "We'll have a party."

"With what?"

"Oh, I'll sell something." She looked around vaguely. "I'll ask Stokes. He's awfully clever at selling things." Stokes was the butler. "Have some champagne, dear. This calls for a celebration."

So the earl took champagne and stayed drinking with his wife until Lucy returned and said acidly that they had better both go and lie down or they would be as drunk as sailors at the Chadburys' dinner.

Unlike the earl's castle, Appleton House, home of the Chadburys, was relatively modern with a fine Palladian front looking out over landscaped gardens and was a good two miles from the sea. But when she was younger, Isabella had always envied Lucy. It seemed much more exciting to live in a ruin of a castle on the edge of the cliffs.

Mr. and Mrs. Chadbury had exquisite taste. The tall, cool rooms were filled with the finest furniture, paintings, sculpture, and objects d'art.

The earl and his family had been invited to come at five o'clock to sit down to dinner at six, the Chadburys feeling that the new fashionable dinner hour in town of seven o'clock was just too late for the country. Isabella and her parents were seated on a long terrace at the front of the house, awaiting the arrival of their guests.

"How odd!" remarked Isabella. "I see them in the distance. They are on foot! And they appear to be punching one other."

It had all been the earl's fault. He had declared that they were all losing the use of their limbs by driving here and there in carriages. Horses and carriages were a needless expense, and so they should walk the ten miles to Appleton House.

The countess would never have agreed had she remembered it was ten whole miles. The day was fine, and they set out with a cursing and grumbling old retainer carrying the lamp that was to light their way home. After five miles, the countess began to complain that her feet hurt. She was wearing old-fashioned shoes with high red heels which, her husband was quick to point out, were the problem and *not* the distance.

"Do so be the gurt distance," moaned the old retainer, "and a curse be on you and yours."

Lucy swung round. "Shut your mouth you old fool or I will shut it for you," she snapped. She marched on but pretended not to notice when a clod of earth thrown by the enraged old retainer went whistling past her ear. The servants had not been paid for ages, so as the countess pointed out, one must allow them their little grumbles and foibles.

They were just approaching Appleton House when the earl began to whimper. "I have *corns*. Bless me, why did I ever think of this scheme?"

"Yes, why did you?" the countess demanded, punching him on the arm.

"Gurt old fool," muttered the old retainer. Lucy, who would not take any criticism of her father from anyone other than her mother, kicked the old retainer in the shins, and then ran to catch up with her parents who were now running toward the house, both having decided that was a good way to shorten the distance.

The old retainer stumbled after them, stooping occasionally to pick up stones and turf to throw at them and fortunately missing every time.

"Oh, heaven!" cried the countess, sinking down into a chair on the terrace beside Mrs. Chadbury. "My poor broken feet. My darling, Sophia," to Mrs. Chadbury, "get one of your well-trained minions to fetch me a bowl of mustard and water for my feet."

"That's for colds," Isabella said, highly amused.

"No, no, my duck. Mustard and water for the feet

and brandy for the inside of me, and I shall be a new woman."

Isabella tried not to laugh as a bowl of water and mustard was placed at the countess's feet. Lady Tremayne kicked off her high heels, pulled off her stockings, deposited a pair of worn red garters on the table, and sank her feet into the water with a loud "Aaah!" of pleasure.

The old retainer tottered forward and helped himself to a glass of brandy.

"That's a bit forward of him," remarked Isabella.

"Horrible old thing, isn't he?" said Lucy. "But he's been with the family for years and hasn't been paid in ages, so we let him have a lot of license. Oh, you'll never guess. Part of the east wing fell into the sea last night."

"What on earth happened?"

"Part of the cliff fell away."

"But, my dear Lucy. Your life may be in danger."

"Not yet. My apartments are in the west wing."

Isabella looked at Lucy with affection. Lucy's face was shiny, and her gown was shabby. Her hair was frizzy and auburn, and her face was dusted with freckles. She lay back in her chair comfortably while Isabella sat bolt upright as she had been trained to do by a severe governess. Miss Chadbury, a lady's back should never touch the back of the chair!

The air was warm and sweet and smelled of roses and newly cut grass. Bats fluttered about overhead in the twilight, and Lucy thought it odd that bats should fly about Appleton House instead of round Tregar Castle, her crumbling family home.

She became aware that her parents and Mr. and Mrs. Chadbury were rising to their feet.

"Dinner?" she asked.

"Not yet," said Mrs. Chadbury. "You girls stay here. We have business to discuss."

"What business, I wonder," Lucy mused when they had gone inside. "Papa cannot be asking your father for money because he never asks people he likes for money. What was the Season like?"

"The same as last one," said Isabella. "Hot rooms and hot gentlemen."

"Didn't you have a beau?"

"Plenty of beaux, but none suitable."

"I should not be so hard to please," said Lucy. "Only I couldn't bear one of those Nonpareils, you know, all elegance and manners. He would scare me to death."

"I don't like fops either," said Isabella.

"What kind of man *do* you like, Isabella? We all dream."

Isabella smiled, a little sad smile, "Oh, I have dreams of my own. I would like to live here until the end of my days, unwed."

"Oh, Isabella. Why?"

"Why not? I have a very good life. I wonder what our parents are talking about?"

"So that's settled," said Mr. Chadbury. "Lord Harry will marry Isabella. Our lawyers will get together tomorrow. Here is a miniature of Isabella to send to Lord Harry. Are you sure he will want this marriage?"

"He'll do what he's told," said the countess ruthlessly. "He knows we need money. Besides, he's thirty. Hasn't shown a fancy for anyone before this."

"He cannot have had much opportunity," said Mrs. Chadbury doubtfully. "He joined the army at fifteen and he's been at one war or another ever since."

"I don't think Isabella is going to like this," remarked the countess, ignoring Mrs. Chadbury's remarks about her son.

"Oh, well," said Mr. Chadbury, "she is just going to have to like it, is she not? Shall we go in to dinner?"

Isabella, unaware of her fate, enjoyed that dinner party. She had never seen the earl and countess in such high spirits before. Lucy, like her parents, ate a vast amount of the delicious food before her, although she privately decided that Mr. Chadbury must have given her father some money to cause all this hilarity. She found herself glancing from time to time at the beautiful statue that was Isabella, cool and gracious in white muslin with a gold filet binding her hair. She had wanted to ask Isabella to go looking for gulls' eggs on the cliffs with her on the following day but somehow felt that one could not ask a fashionplate to do anything so vulgar. But perhaps that would happen to her in another couple of years. Perhaps she, too, would become graceful and elegant. But graceful and elegant people did not seem to have any fun. Isabella was enjoying the company, but Lucy sensed a coldness in her.

"Harry's coming home," she said to Isabella. "I

wonder what he's like now. I saw him five years ago. He's old now, of course. Thirty! Fancy being thirty!"

"Thirty is a mature age," said the countess and gave Mrs. Chadbury a vulgar wink.

At last, the Tremaynes rose to leave. The old retainer was found lying drunk on the terrace, an empty brandy bottle beside him.

"Silly old fool," said Lucy impatiently. "He'll kill himself if he goes on drinking like that."

"You musn't walk," said Mrs. Chadbury. "We're having the carriage brought round for you. I insist."

"Oh, do, do insist," said the countess gratefully. She looked down at the old servant. "What are we to do with what's his name? Put him in the basket?"—meaning the long basket slung behind carriages for luggage.

"We can't do that," said Lucy. "He'll roll about and break his neck. He'll just need to travel inside with us and lie along the seat where we can hold him."

And so as Lucy pushed her feet against the recumbent body of the drunken old retainer so that he would not roll off the seat in the carriage, she asked her parents why they were so merry.

"We've arranged a marriage," crowed the countess. "Isabella and our Harry. The Chadburys have been most generous, in fact part of the arrangement is that you are to have a Season when you are nineteen, Lucy."

"Oh, lor' " Lucy frowned. "What's Isabella to say to things?"

"Nothing at all. Her parents have had enough of her playing fast and loose. It's to be an arranged marriage."

"Harry, as I remember," said Lucy, "is not the sort to be ordered around. And Isabella? Goodness, she could have her pick."

"She's had her pick of the best," said the earl happily, "and she didn't want any of them, which is why the Chadburys are arranging a marriage."

"A marriage of inconvenience!" said Lucy, and laughed.

Chapter Two

Known affectionately by the men in his regiment as Lord Harry, Isabella's future husband's title was in fact that of Viscount Tregar as, being the heir to the earldom, he used one of his father's courtesy titles. His rank in the army was that of colonel. But he was rarely called Viscount Tregar, even the Cornish locals referring to him as Lord Harry.

He was a tall, athletic man, careless in his dress and possessing a mischievous nature that he had not outgrown. He accepted everything life sent his way with good nature. He considered his bout of fever extremely good luck, for it had brought him a chance of leave, away from battling with Napoleon's troops. What he also rated as another piece of good fortune was that his best friend, Captain James Godolphin, also a Cornishman, had also caught the fever, and like Lord Harry had recovered on the voyage home. Lord Harry had invited the captain to stay with him at Tregar Castle. The friends were in complete contrast. Lord Harry had thick black curly hair, a strong handsome face, wide blue eyes, and a firm chin. Clothes as far as he was concerned were just things to protect one from the weather. Captain James, on the other hand, was tall, slim and neat, and fanatical about the niceties of dress. He was a brave soldier and yet would never dream of going into battle in an unpressed uniform or unshaved any more than he would have dreamed of turning up at Almack's, say, in anything but the latest fashion. He had blond hair teased into that elaborate style known as the Windswept, and his cravats were a miracle of starched design.

Lord Harry was lounging at his ease in the regiment's mess in Portsmouth opening up the morning's post when he gave a surprised exclamation.

"What's amiss?" asked the captain.

"It seems I am to be married," said Lord Harry, "and here's the bride." He handed Captain James the miniature of Isabella that his father had sent him.

"Goodness, can she possibly really be as beautiful as this?" asked the captain.

"It doesn't matter if she is," said Lord Harry. "She's an heiress, and my parents are in need of funds. They assume I will do my duty. They are going ahead to arrange the marriage."

"A bit high handed that," commented the captain. "What if you don't want the girl?"

"I don't want anyone else. May as well let them get on with it. I'll be going back to the Peninsula soon, so I needn't see much of her, parents get her money and everybody is happy."

"Do be careful. What if you fall in love with someone else after you are married?"

"I won't," said Lord Harry cynically. "I've dealt with all the business here, so we may as well leave right away and get this marriage over with, unless you've got anything to keep you."

"No. But you must allow my man plenty of time to pack. I refuse to turn up in a creased coat."

"You've never been to Tregar Castle, have you James? My parents wouldn't notice if you arrived in your nightshirt."

Lucy rode over to Appleton House on the following day to see Isabella. She was curious to find out how the beauty had taken the news of her arranged marriage.

She was ushered into the drawing room where Isabella was embroidering the bodice of a dress.

"Goodness, it's hot." Lucy sighed, taking off her old straw bonnet and hurling it into a corner. "Well, Isabella, so you are to marry my brother?"

"We will see," said Isabella. "I do not remember your brother, although I must have met him. What is he like?"

"I haven't seem him in ages, but he is great fun and quite good-looking, I think. Very easy going."

"Surely a thirty-year-old man will not wed some girl chosen for him by his parents?"

"Well, Harry's deuced fond of Ma and Pa. The way he'll look at it is that if they need the money, then he may as well go along with the marriage. I mean, it's not as if you want anyone else, Isabella."

"The sad fact is I do not want anyone at all."

"You can't mean that." Lucy rubbed at her nose in the way she always did when she was worried or upset. "I mean, I haven't met anyone yet, but I dream of a beau. I haven't ever been kissed. Have you?"

Isabella repressed a shudder. "No."

"I would like to find out what it's like. I mean, do people tremble with love and go ashen pale like they do in the romances?"

"Probably not." Isabella carefully chose a skein of silk thread.

"But Shakespeare wrote of love, and he was terribly clever. He must have known what he was talking about."

"I do not want to talk of fairy tales," said Isabella. "Let us be practical. Suppose I am pressed into this marriage. What experience has your brother had of polite society?"

"Not much. He left Eton at fifteen and went straight into the army. I read however that Wellington likes his officers to be able to dance properly. He cannot be devoid of the social graces, and why should it matter anyway?"

"I like the elegancies of life," said Isabella. "I detest coarse, loud-voiced men."

"Never mind. Let's go out for a ride. It's a glorious day."

"Why?"

"Why, why . . . why because we can ride like the wind through the countryside in the sunshine."

"What an energetic girl you are! Very well." Isabella stowed away her sewing things neatly. "Wait until I change into a riding dress."

Soon they were riding over the springy turf on the cliffs above the sea. The weather was glorious. Little boats like toys bobbed on the blue sea, and clumps of sea pinks fluttered at the edge of the cliffs on the sage green grass. They were accompanied by two grooms from Appleton House, which Lucy, who rode everywhere on her own, felt restricted their freedom. But Isabella seemed livelier than she had been for a long time.

They reined in their horses on the edge of the cliff. "Of course, if we could find grandfather's treasure, Harry wouldn't need to marry you," said Lucy.

"Oh, that!" Isabella laughed. "Do you remember how when we were children, we searched and searched through the castle. What was the treasure supposed to be? A box of jewels? What romantics we were then!"

"But it's not just a tale," said Lucy eagerly. "There's a portrait of Grandma in the library, and she's simply dripping with jewels."

"Why would your grandfather bother to hide them?" asked Isabella.

"Because he had windmills in his cockloft before he died, and he took against Mama and didn't want her to have them. Perhaps they were buried with him? Perhaps we should dig up his coffin!"

"Nonsense. If they were buried with him then the earl would know about it. We looked everywhere, if you remember."

"But we were terribly young and immature," said seventeen-year-old Lucy. "A systematic search is called for."

"Another day," said Isabella and turned her mount toward home.

The ride with Lucy had done her good, and Isabella decided she had not been firm enough about this marriage. She sought out her parents who had just returned from a visit to their lawyers and said, "This has got to stop. I am not going to marry Lord Harry, and that is that."

Her parents looked at her coldly. "For once," said her father evenly, "you will do as you are told. That is an end of the matter."

In vain did Isabella plead. Her usually indulgent parents had grown hard and adamant.

Her mind twisted this way and that, trying to find an escape. The old earl's treasure might be an answer . . . if it still existed, and Isabella was sure it did not.

Captain James eyed the bulk of Tregar Castle nervously. It appeared to be hanging onto the edge of the cliff. "Do my eyes deceive me," he said, "or has a bit of it fallen off?"

"Yes, it has," said Lord Harry. "My father told me that a bit of the east wing had dropped into the sea. I'm afraid our rooms are in the east wing—or what's left of it—so if you hear a rumble in the night, you'd best be smartish about getting out."

The castle door was opened to them by an elderly butler. "Here I am, Stokes," said Lord Harry cheerfully. "Turned up again like the proverbial bad penny."

The butler grunted by way of reply.

The captain removed his hat and gloves and held them out. The butler ignored them.

"Leave them on the side table, James," said Lord Harry.

27

"Why doesn't this servant take them?" asked the captain.

"Why should I?" demanded the butler passionately. "Mark my words, the day will come when the likes o' you will be hanging from the lantern."

"Quite right, Stokes," said Lord Harry amiably. "Come along, James."

The captain took out his pocket handkerchief and pointedly dusted the side table before putting down his hat and gloves. Then he followed Lord Harry, his impeccably tailored back stiff with outrage.

"This is your room, James," said Lord Harry, kicking open a door in the middle of a passage.

The room was cold and dark. Ivy grew thickly over the mullioned window. Two elderly footmen came in carrying the captain's bags.

The captain struck the bedcovers with the flat of his hand. A cloud of dust rose and then hung in the air.

"I do not mean to criticize your hospitality," said the captain coldly, "but I would like clean blankets and linen."

The two footmen cackled wildly as if he had said something very funny.

"Don't look so outraged, James. They've got out of the way of service for the simple reason they probably haven't been paid for years."

James looked horrified. "But one should always pay one's servants. Why did you not let me bring my man with me? I have an idea." He said to one of the footmen. "Fetch that butler here . . . Stokes."

"What are you going to do?" asked Lord Harry. "Horsewhip the lot of 'em?"

"Just watch."

Stokes creaked in. "What does ee want?" he demanded.

James took several guineas out of his pocket and began to toss them up and down. "Gold, old man," he said, "which will be paid to you to distribute among the staff if this room is cleaned and aired, the ivy stripped from outside the window, and washing water brought to the toilet table."

The butler bowed low. "Certainly, master," he quavered.

"I'll move into your room while they get busy with mine," said James. "Really, Harry, badly treated servants always behave badly. You should know that."

"Tell my parents. Here's my quarters along from yours. I hope you're right in telling them to cut the ivy away from the window. I'm sure it's what holds this castle up."

The door opened, and the elderly retainer creaked in. Lord Harry greeted him warmly. His name was Biddle, and Lord Harry could never remember him having looked any younger or having any specific job, although he wore the indoor livery of a footman.

"Hey, Biddle," cried Lord Harry. "Here I am, back home."

"Them's gone to Appleton House, and you and the gennelmun here is to go fer dinner."

Lord Harry raised his eyebrows. "So I am to meet my bride so soon. What's she like, Biddle?"

"Fair as the flower o' May and as cold as charity," said the old man.

"How would you know if she's cold?"

"Cos when she passes un, there's a cold wind."

"Fustian. Well, come along, James. We'll ride over. Put your evening dress in a saddle bag. Don't look like that, man. Neither the Chadburys nor my parents will remark if your coat is creased."

The castle, reflected James as they rode off, looked better in the distance, its gray towers softened by the mellow light. It was not a large castle, had no moat or portcullis, but it looked as if it had stood for centuries. James wondered how Lord Harry could bear to see his family home descending into the sea, bit by bit, and yet he envied his friend his insouciance. He himself could not bear a household of such weird servants, nor could he ride easily out to meet a future bride. He was obsessive about manners and appearance, and yet, as he rode through the lazy Cornish countryside, he wondered for the first time why he should control his life with so many finicky little taboos. What would it be like to be like Lord Harry? Happy, he thought suddenly.

"We'll leave the horses at the stables and walk up," called Lord Harry as Appleton House came into sight.

This was more like it, thought James, as a correct groom said their bags would be carried up to the house.

"Beautiful place, isn't it?" said Lord Harry. "But almost too perfect. Let me show you the rose garden. Round the side here and through the little gate. There! What do you think of that?"

Roses rioted over trellises and from urns, filling the air with their heady scent. Somewhere a thrush sang and then fell silent. "Home in England again, hey, James?" said Lord Harry softly.

"And that," said the captain quietly, "if I am not mistaken, is your future bride." He pointed toward the house. The Green Saloon overlooked the rose garden. Standing, framed in the window, was Isabella. Both men recognized her from her miniature. "Move closer," muttered Lord Harry. "I want to get a better look at her before we're introduced."

They moved quietly forward through the roses. Lord Harry realized Isabella was talking to his parents.

Her cool voice reached their ears. "So, Lord and Lady Tremayne," said Isabella, "as I am being forced into marriage with your son, may I point out to you that as he left school and went straight into the army, he must be in need of some town bronze, some refinement. To that end, I suggest we introduce him to London society. You would not have me marry some uncouth lout I take it? May I beg the marriage is delayed until after the Little Season so that he may be allowed to experience some civilizing influences?"

Lord Harry tugged James's arm and drew him back. "I have a plan," he whispered, his eyes dancing. "I'll give the minx what she wants. We'll say we do not want to be announced yet. I'll tell you what I have in mind when we're inside."

"So what's the plan?" said James, looking around the well-appointed bedroom with pleasure. There was a new bed with brocade curtains hanging from a central coronet. Curtains of finest Brussels lace

31

fluttered lazily at the long windows. An exquisite little nosegay of flowers had been placed on a table beside the bed.

"I am going to be a veritable Pink of the Ton," said Lord Harry gleefully. "I am going to mince and scrape and bow and treat Miss Isabella as if I find her the veriest provincial. To that end, I need to borrow your clothes, my peacock."

"But your shoulders are broader than mine, and you'll ruin my coats!"

"With your fortune, James, you can replace them. You have often offered me money, and I have always refused. It will be like charades. You act like me for a change. Do you good."

James hesitated. Had he not been envying his friends carelessness earlier on? James had always worked to keep up appearances. Even after a bloody battle when all his comrades were lying about exhausted, Captain James Godolphin sat in the middle of them, carefully brushing his uniform. He had even invented a concoction for removing bloodstains. But just for a little, just to relax . . .

"Very well," he said.

"Right. But I need paint and powder."

"I have some hair powder. Paint? I do not paint, Harry."

"My mother does. I wonder if she's brought her toilet case along. I'll go on a raid. Back in a minute."

After a while Lord Harry returned, triumphant. "Good old, Mama. Look at this. Blanc and rouge and some vile perfume, too. Here's my traps, James, and I'll take yours. Wait until you see the finished man."

James unpacked Lord Harry's evening wear and, after a wash, put it on. It hung slightly loosely on him, particularly about the shoulders, but it felt amazingly comfortable. He brushed out his hairstyle, the Windswept, and then combed it back into a simple fashion.

An hour later, Lord Harry appeared in all his glory, and James laughed out loud. Lord Harry now had *his* hair teased and curled into the Windswept. His face was covered in white blanc with two circles of rouge on his cheeks. James's dark blue evening coat was strained across his shoulders, and James's breeches on Lord Harry's thighs were tight to the point of indecency. His watch chain was decorated with seals and fobs. He carried a large lace-edged handkerchief in one hand and a vinaigrette in the other.

"What do you think?" he asked, twirling about.

"Horrible. Don't you want to marry her?"

"Not much. I'll probably have to, all the same. Let's go down."

The Chadburys and Tremaynes waited impatiently in the drawing room. Dinner had been put back an hour. "What can be keeping them?" asked Lady Tremayne anxiously. "It's not as if Harry ever bothers about dress."

Lucy, for her part, envied Isabella's calm. The servants had said her brother had brought a friend with him. Would this prove to be the man of her dreams? Possibly not. Harry was thirty, and so it

33

followed that his friend was probably old as well. She noticed a wine stain on the bodice of her dress and dabbed at it with a grubby handkerchief. "Try spitting on your handkerchief," said her mother.

"Seltzer is the best thing," said Isabella. She carried over a small bottle of seltzer, soaked her own clean handkerchief with it, and then efficiently began to remove the stain from Lucy's dress.

"Viscount Tregar and Captain James Godolphin," announced the butler.

Isabella stood frozen, the seltzer soaked handkerchief in one hand. Lucy whispered, "Oh, dear." The earl and countess stared, their mouths open, while Mr. and Mrs. Chadbury looked at each other in despair. Then the tableau broke up. The countess rose to her feet and darted to her son and flung her arms around him. "Harry, oh, dear Harry."

He put her gently aside and said in a rather high, precise voice, "Do be careful of Weston's tailoring, Mama."

"Why, Harry! How you have changed. So this is your friend? Charmed." The countess looked flustered. "You know the Chadburys, of course, and this, my dear, is Isabella."

Lord Harry bowed so low his nose nearly touched the ground. He waved his handkerchief in a series of elaborate swoops.

Then he straightened up and raised a quizzing glass and studied his bride to be from the top of her burnished curls to her small and dainty feet.

"You *might* do," he said. "A little town bronze needed, I think."

"Isabella has had two Seasons in London," commented her father stiffly.

"Indeed!" Lord Harry walked slowly around Isabella as if examining a statue. "And she did not take?"

"On the contrary," exclaimed his mother. "Isabella received many proposals of marriage."

"Stap me! Never would have believed it!"

"Harry," snapped his father. "Stop prancing around like a coxcomb and mind your manners."

Lord Harry sat down after carefully raising the skirts of his coat. James, attempting his new role, lounged back in a chair next to him.

"So tell me how the war goes," said the earl. "Will we defeat Boney, think you?"

"Tut, tut," reproved his son. "Ladies present." He turned to Isabella. "I must have new gloves made. I believe lavender is the latest color."

"Yes, for ladies," said Lucy.

"Nonetheless, I think lavender would suit me very well." He began to discourse on glove makers in that new high mincing voice of his until Mrs. Chadbury said in desperation that they should all go in for dinner.

James found he was sorry for Isabella. She was trying to mask her horror, but her beautiful eyes kept straying in Lord Harry's direction as if looking at some species of loathsome insect. He found himself seated next to Lady Lucy. She was a pleasing, if messy, child, he considered as he amiably stooped several times to retrieve her napkin. "We don't have these new things at the castle," said

Lucy. "We just wipe our mouths on the tablecloth in the good old English way."

James repressed a shudder. His man carried clean table linen as well as clean everything else for his master, even to the battlefront.

Lord Harry was describing a play the officers had put on in Lisbon. "I was most effective," he said. "I played the wronged virgin. You should have heard Wellington laugh. He said I had the neatest ankles he had ever seen."

The countess took a deep breath. She wanted to scream at her son and then tell him the marriage was off. But they needed the money so desperately. And who was ever going to please Isabella?

"Poor Isabella," said Lucy to James. "Who would ever have thought my brother would turn out to be a fop. How does he fight anyone?"

"Oh, he's very brave," said James.

"Such a pity we can't find Grandpapa's treasure," mourned Lucy. "For then we should be rich, and Harry would not need to marry Isabella."

"Tell me about this treasure."

"Well, Grandpapa was very much in love with Grandmama, and *she* was fond of diamonds, and so he bought her the best. When she died, I think his brain became somewhat addled. He took a dislike to Mama, who should have got the jewels, and said she would never have them. Then when Grandpapa died, we found he had hidden them somewhere. We never could find them."

He smiled at her, thinking her a nice little thing. He liked her freckles and her fuzzy, frizzy auburn hair.

"Perhaps you did not look hard enough," he volunteered. "Some of these old buildings have hidden rooms and priest holes and things like that. Have you any plans of the castle?"

"I have never seen any," said Lucy. "The castle is really not so very old. But mayhap they did not need plans but just sort of threw buildings up."

"Even then, they had plans or blueprints or something. Would you like me to help you look?"

"Oh, yes," said Lucy. She thought he was nice, so much nicer than Harry. She liked his fair hair and his gray eyes. He could not be a stickler for dress for his coat was quite loose, and so he surely would not despise her shabby gown. "When can we start?"

"We'll see. Perhaps tomorrow."

"May I . . . may I ask you something?"

"It depends on what it is."

"Well, I shall ask you just the same. I have not seen Harry in five years, but I remember clearly he was easy going then and not at all high in the instep. He is making a cake of himself and giving Isabella a disgust of him. He has changed terribly."

"Perhaps he is nervous," said James. "It is a marriage of convenience, after all."

Mrs. Chadbury finally rose to lead the ladies to the drawing room. To the earl's irritation, his son suggested the gentlemen join them. The earl had been hoping to have some more of Mr. Chadbury's excellent port.

When they reached the drawing room, Lord Harry said to Mrs. Chadbury, "Perhaps my betrothed would like to show me the rose garden."

"It's as black as pitch out there," protested the earl.

"There is still some light," drawled Lord Harry.

"Go ahead," said Mrs. Chadbury with a sigh.

As Lord Harry escorted Isabella out into the garden, he could feel her whole body shrinking away from him. He reflected he had never seen so beautiful a woman before, or such a cold one. There was still a pale light in the sky. The evening was fine, and the rose garden was dark and shadowy and mysterious, made for love and assignations, he thought.

Isabella described the roses and when they had been planted. He stopped at a sundial in the middle of the garden and turned to face her.

"I would like to remind you," he said haughtily, "that ours is to be a marriage of convenience, if you take my meaning."

"I am being forced to marry you, if that is what you mean," said Isabella, averting her face.

"Dear me, how coarse and insensitive the modern woman is. I shall be more plain. I do not want children."

"Sir, I fail to—"

"To put it even more bluntly, as you seem to be monstrous short of understanding, I do not wish you to inflict the pleasures of the marriage bed on me."

Isabella bit back a hysterical laugh.

"I? Surely, my lord, it is the lady who usually shrinks from intimacy."

His eyes gleamed in the dark. "If you are going to force yourself on me, madam," he said in his mincing voice, "then I must decline your offer."

"Force ... Really, my lord, the facts are these. My parents want me to marry anyone, and you happen to be available. Your parents want money. That is all there is to it."

"You say that now," he said sadly. "But, pon rep, the ladies sigh after me."

"Rest assured, my lord, I cannot imagine sighing after you. In fact, if ours is to be a marriage in name only, then I must admit I can face it with a certain amount of hope. Do your parents really need money so badly?"

"Yes."

Isabella noticed a huge yellow moon was rising. The air was heavily sweet with the scent of roses. It was a night made for romance, she suddenly thought, and then wondered why she should be entertaining such mawkish ideas.

Some imp prompted her to say, "Are you not supposed to get down on one knee and propose to me?"

"And dirty my breeches? No, indeed. Our lawyers, I assume, have already done that for me. We will be married after the Little Season, for I have a mind to enjoy the pleasures of London. Do you always wear white?"

"Usually. It is correct for young, unmarried ladies to wear white."

"Tedious. You should wear colors. I shall introduce you to some good mercers in London."

"How do you know good mercers in London if you have spent all your time at the wars?"

"You do not think I would have my waistcoats purchased in some heathen land?"

"Neither the Spanish nor the Portuguese are heathens."

"In manners of cloth and dress, they are."

"So you worship at the altar of fashion."

"No," said Lord Harry calmly. "Fashion worships me. I shall dazzle the ton in London."

"You know, it is said in the best circles of London that I am an extremely beautiful woman," said Isabella, hoping to goad him.

"You amaze me. You are passable, I admit. But you lack animation or warmth."

"Something that a man milliner like yourself knows all about?"

"You are rude, and yet I speak the truth. Beauty without spirit is an empty shell."

"I think we should go indoors, my lord. I am bored. I beg you to reconsider. You will not be happy with me."

"I do not plan to spend much time in your company, and I shall enjoy your fortune immensely," said Lord Harry. He suddenly screamed and grabbed her arms.

"What is it?" cried Isabella.

"Those black things overhead!"

Isabella firmly disengaged herself. "Bats, my lord. Only bats."

She walked away from him, and he followed more slowly, a smile on his face. Isabella evidently did not know that London gossip reached the battlefields of Spain, and he had suddenly recollected tales of an Isabella, "the fairest in London town," who had a bad reputation for breaking hearts. There was no danger of his falling in love with her any more than there was any danger of his falling in love with a statue.

As he entered the drawing room behind Isabella, he saw his little sister, Lucy, regarding him with mournful disappointment and felt a stab of conscience. Isabella sat down on the sofa next to Lucy, and soon both were engaged in a whispered conversation.

"I know he is your brother," said Isabella, "but he is a coxcomb, a fop."

"I do not know what has happened to him," muttered Lucy. "We must find that treasure. When does he want to marry you?"

"After the Little Season."

"That's what *you* wanted," Lucy pointed out.

"I thought he might need some town bronze, and now it appears he thinks I am in need of it. Fool!"

"Don't you want to marry him?"

"You know I don't, although things are not so bad as I feared. It is to be a marriage in name only."

Lucy wrinkled her brow. "I must think of a plan. I know, he is become so very precious-perfect that if perhaps you were to adopt the manners of a hoyden, then he might not want you at any price."

Isabella's eyes gleamed. "He accused me of being devoid of animation. That would really teach him a lesson. But it is not in me to behave badly."

"Try. We are going treasure hunting tomorrow, and that nice Captain James has promised to help. Wear your old clothes—"

"I do not have any old clothes."

"Well, wear something you won't mind getting

dirty and ... laugh a lot in a boisterous way and slouch and spill things."

Isabella thought this was quite a good description of Lucy herself. In that case she could use Lucy as a model.

"I'll try," she said. "What time?"

"Come early. About eleven in the morning will do. But come alone. Ride over and leave that retinue of servants of yours behind for once!"

Chapter Three

*L*ORD HARRY AWOKE early. Another fine day. His sister had told him on the road home the evening before about the treasure hunt. So Isabella would be arriving at eleven. What a cold fish she was, he thought with amusement. Did he mean to marry her? He could not really see anything against it. He would go back to his regiment after a comfortably long leave. Such as Isabella would never dream of following the drum. In fact, he would not need to see much of her at all.

Had she been a warm-blooded girl who was being forced into an unwelcome marriage, then he would have told his parents to drop the whole idea. But he knew Isabella's reputation. It had all come back to him when he had seen her. She was a cold-hearted flirt, and Lord Harry detested flirts.

He got up and washed and dressed in Captain James's clothes, groaning to himself as he applied paint to his face. But the masquerade must go on. He did not feel bad about tricking his parents. They had always been wrapped up in each other and in their own lives, lives in which he had played very

43

little part. But he was sorry for Lucy and wondered whether he might trust her with his secret.

He knew it was no use trying to rouse the servants. They were all elderly men. The earl and countess did not like women servants. All the servants had been drunk since they got the money from Captain James and were sleeping off the effects.

He went down to the cavernous black castle kitchens and made himself a breakfast of bread, cold ham, and beer, and then he decided to go out for a walk.

The air was like champagne, and the turf beyond the castle walls, springy under his feet. He walked for a long time along the edge of the cliffs, then turned inland. Larks sang in the pure air, high above his head, their trilling songs cascading down to the ground. At last he took out his watch and noted that it was already half past ten. Time to return.

Isabella's parents were not awake when she set off. But the head groom was shocked when she announced her plan to ride to Tregar Castle unescorted. What could happen on such a fine day? protested Isabella. She knew everyone for miles around. She was in no danger. The head groom reminded her of what was due to her consequence, but the new Isabella, dressed in a rather worn, short, tight riding dress that she had found in a trunk and had not worn for three years, said she did not give a fig for consequence. Stubbornly, the man said he could not allow it, it would be more than his job was worth.

Isabella turned on her heel and strode off, but instead of returning to the house, she looped the train of her riding dress over her arm and set out to walk on foot to Tregar Castle.

Lord Rupert Fitzjohn, seated on his horse on a small rise that commanded the surrounding countryside, could not believe his luck when he saw Isabella Chadbury walking unescorted along a dusty road that led away from her home. Every day, he had ridden from the inn where he was staying under an assumed name to just this point, watching and waiting for an opportunity. He had been there the day before with his small telescope, through which he had witnessed the arrival of the earl and countess and their daughter. He had seen two men riding up later. Still, he had remained at his post until darkness fell.

His lips curled in a smile. He had her at last. He put the telescope in his saddlebag and then drew a soft black mask out of his pocket and put it on so that most of his face was covered. Then he spurred his horse forward and down toward the road.

He reined in behind Isabella and dismounted. She turned curiously, at first unafraid, expecting to see one of her neighbors. Her eyes widened in alarm as she saw the mask. She looked wildly to left and right, but there was no one to be seen. He strolled toward her as she stood rigid with fear in the middle of the road.

And then she found her voice and screamed and screamed.

Lord Harry, ambling along, heard that scream and broke into a run, fobs and seals bobbing, cursing his constricting finery.

He bounded over the turf and came in sight of the road. A woman had been seized by a masked man, and he was dragging her to a ditch at the side of the road.

As he got closer, he recognized Isabella. "Hey!" he shouted.

The masked man released Isabella and whipped round. Lord Harry stopped and picked up a stone that was lying nearby. He threw it with unerring aim, and it struck the masked stranger full on the forehead. He reeled back, stumbled, regained his balance and before Lord Harry could reach him, he had run to his horse, swung himself into the saddle, and ridden off.

"Damn," muttered Lord Harry and then strolled to where Isabella was crouched in the ditch. "I' Faith, Miss Isabella," he drawled, "you brought that upon yourself. No groom or footman!"

Isabella glared at him. She carefully extricated her hair, which had become caught in the long spiny tendrils of a blackberry bush, and crawled out of the ditch. Anger at him was driving out fear, and she had been most terribly afraid. "Such a thing has never happened before. Never!"

He surveyed her thoughtfully. Her hair was tousled for her hat had come off in the struggle and the tightness of her old dress showed the heavings of her bosom. His eye traveled down to the skirt which, despite the dusty train at the back, was too short in the front. Yes, her ankles were excellent. Such a pity her soul was a mess.

"I shall escort you to Tregar Castle," said Lord Harry. "My sister will attend to you. Perhaps you should lie down in a darkened room and await the physician. I shall deal with the authorities, who must be summoned. Are you well enough to walk or shall I carry you?"

"I am perfectly well, if shaken," said Isabella firmly.

"So glad," he said seriously, "for you are quite a strapping wench, and it would indeed be an effort to have to carry you. My clothes are already suffering from the ungentlemanly exercise. There is nothing worse than an excess of vigor for spoiling the line of one's coat. Do you know the identity of your assailant?"

"No, he must have been some drunk or madman. There are footpads on the roads nearer the larger towns, but I have never heard of any in this vicinity."

"Footpad? He was wearing a fine blue coat and breeches of doeskin. His horse was a showy beast."

"I know all the gentlemen for miles around," said Isabella, walking along beside him. "None would behave in such a manner."

There was a silence, and then Lord Harry said, "As far as I could see, he was intent on rape rather than robbery."

"My lord!"

"He was, wasn't he?"

Isabella remembered the assailant's hand, which had fumbled in the front of her dress while the other held her tightly against him. She shuddered and stopped, her face quite white as the shock of the attack hit her at last.

"You may cry on my shoulder if you like." Lord Harry's voice was mocking.

Color flooded into her cheeks, and she walked on. "I am quite recovered, my lord."

Lord Harry had meant to anger her, for he did not want her to go into hysterics or faint.

When they arrived at the castle, Lucy came running out to meet them, dressed in a neat and clean gown and with pretty blue ribbons in her hair. As if remembering her new role of lady, she stopped before she reached them. Ladies, Lucy knew, did not run or bounce or show any excitement.

"You had best get Father," said Lord Harry. "Miss Isabella was attacked on her way here."

"Attacked? Oh, this is terrible." Lucy put an arm around Isabella's shoulders. "You poor thing."

Isabella could feel tears welling up in her eyes, but she was determined not to cry before Lord Harry, and it was only when Lucy had guided her into the morning room that she broke down and sobbed. Lucy, with a wisdom beyond her years, sat silently next to her and let her cry. At last Isabella dried her eyes and gave Lucy a shaky smile. "I cannot remember crying like that since I was a child," she said. "But why should anyone attack me in broad daylight? I am lucky Lord Harry came on the scene and scared that dreadful man away."

"So Harry is not entirely a fop?"

"He threw a stone at him, but other than that he did not have to do anything. He complained the exercise in running to rescue me had spoiled the line of his coat."

"Oh, dear," said Lucy. "My brother is past redemption."

She might have changed her mind if she could have seen Lord Harry organizing a search for the assailant with military precision. The colonel of the local militia and his men had been called in. Lord Harry gave them a concise description of the assailant's build, height, clothes, and horse.

Mr. and Mrs. Chadbury arrived and rushed to see their daughter. By afternoon the countryside was alive with searching men, and the treasure hunt had been forgotten. By evening, they had discovered that a man wearing the clothes that Lord Harry had described and riding a horse that also matched his description had been staying at The George, an inn at the nearest large town of Dowlas along the coast, under the name of Mr. Sand. He had left that day in a great hurry.

"What do you think?" Captain James asked Lord Harry. "Some madman? And yet the landlord describes him as a gentleman, but cannot add much to your description except that he was 'quite handsome.' "

They were strolling through what passed for gardens around the castle, unkempt grass that was cropped by lazy sheep.

"I think perhaps it was one of Miss Isabella's rejects. She must have wounded many souls during her two Seasons. It may sound cruel, but it did her some good, I think. She actually came to life."

49

"Yes, you do sound cruel. Such a thing to happen to a gently reared female is appalling."

"An appalling thing to happen to any female, be she scullery maid or duchess," Lord Harry pointed out. "A low station in society does not necessarily mean the woman is devoid of feeling."

Captain James eyed his friend uneasily. "You sound like a Whig."

Lord Harry laughed. "The worst thing to sound like in your book. Dinner should be ready soon, and I am sharp set, although one look at the table usually cures that."

"Oh, dear, do your parents not keep a good table?"

"They keep a very bad table. I should have warned you."

To Lord Harry's surprise, as they entered one of the small dark rooms that was ambitiously called the White Saloon for the walls were grimy with two centuries of smoke and dust, he noticed that Isabella was still wearing her riding dress whereas his hoydenish sister was attired in a silk gown. Captain James, too, noticed that silk gown particularly. It was of soft green silk with the low neckline ornamented with a fall of fine lace.

Lucy had suddenly declared she wanted to dress properly for dinner, and Isabella, glad to have something to take her mind off her bad experience, had appealed to the countess. The countess had produced an old silk gown of her own, along with a box of fine lace, and Isabella had worked to transform the dress to fit Lucy and then to stitch the lace onto the neckline.

Lord Harry raised his quizzing glass. "You are looking remarkably bon ton, Lucy."

"Yes, she is," remarked Mrs. Chadbury with an edge to her voice. "I wish I could say the same for my daughter. Why you are so determined to sit down to dinner in that disgraceful old riding dress is beyond me, Isabella. We are allowing you license this evening because of what happened today. But never insult your host and hostess again by sitting down to dinner looking like a guy."

Isabella flushed. "I don't know," said Lord Harry, putting his head on one side and surveying the blushing Isabella. "Diana, chaste and fair. Nothing like riding dress for showing off the female form."

"Stop giving poor Isabella a jaw-me-dead, all of you." Lucy was bristling with temper. "Has she not endured enough?"

"Her day of misery is not over yet," drawled Lord Harry. "For I suppose you still have old Fotheringay as chef in the kitchen."

The earl looked surprised. "Of course. No one can deal with roast beef like old Fotheringay."

"True," murmured Lord Harry. "Sad, but true."

His mother rose to her feet and walked over to him. She took hold of his quizzing glass, which was hanging round his neck by a gold chain, and held the glass up to what light there was coming in through the ivy-covered window.

"This is plain glass," she said. "What's the point of it all?"

Captain James laughed. "It is a dangerous weapon. The quizzing glass, Countess, is not to see with. It is to glare through, to freeze, to disarm one's enemies, to repel the advances of mushrooms and counter-jumpers. The same applies to the snuff box. Many gentlemen carry snuff boxes but do not take snuff themselves. The box demonstrates the wealth of the owner—the way he flicks the lid and offers a pinch, his breeding; the mixture, his good taste."

"Sounds like a lot of rot to me," remarked the countess.

"Which will probably describe the dinner we are about to have," murmured Lord Harry as his mother moved off toward the dining room on his father's arm.

The earl did not believe in all this newfangled nonsense of having servants hand round dishes. Everything was placed in front of him, and he carved and filled the plates and passed them along. Ladies, too, had to know how to carve as well, and Isabella had been taught at special carving lessons in London, the price being a guinea a lesson.

She had learned the different carving terms. You break a deer, rear a goose, lift a swan, spoil a hen, disfigure a peacock, allay a pheasant, thigh a pigeon, unjoint a bittern, chine a salmon, splatt a pike, splay a bream, side a haddock, culpon a trout, and barbe a lobster.

Isabella found herself praying there would be no roast beef, for the castle roast beef always arrived at the table oozing blood from every pore. She often wondered if the chef just waved it over the fire and then brought it upstairs. Lucy had pointed out that afternoon that as ladies were expected to eat like birds, then Isabella, if she wished to offend Lord

Harry, should learn to eat heartily. But not this dinner, thought Isabella. The food was either burned to a crisp or not cooked at all. Her worst fears were realized after the buttock of beef was carried in and proceeded to squirt fountains of blood when the earl thrust his carving fork into it. Perhaps there should be a new carving term added to the list, thought Isabella—cannibalizing a buttock of beef.

"Remember that chap who attended a dinner at the Beefsteak Club in London?" asked Lord Harry. "He said it was an appalling sight. He said he half expected them to start carving up each other."

Isabella concentrated on eating the vegetables on her dish, those that were not soaked in blood.

She suddenly had an idea how she might rile Lord Harry. He wanted a marriage in which he would see as little of her as possible. She smiled at him, and said, "When we are married, I shall of course, go everywhere with you."

Lord Harry looked at her in surprise. "As soon as we are married," he said gently, "I shall be returning to Portugal and then to Spain."

"So I shall follow the drum," said Isabella gaily.

"Isabella!" shrieked her mother.

Even Captain James looked horrified. "It is no life for a lady, Miss Isabella," he said.

"But last Season I was talking to Lady Terry and she had just returned from the wars and told me of the balls and parties."

"We do have balls and parties and amateur theatricals," said Captain James. "But such pleasures are few and far between. Have you thought of the discomfort, of the long route marches, of the abysmal sleeping quarters?"

Lord Harry smiled. "Besides, it takes a certain type of lady."

"Explain," snapped Isabella, angry to see that she had only succeeded in amusing him.

"Well, there is the famous case of Juana Maria de Los Deloros de Leon."

"Do tell me about her."

"It was after the siege of Badajoz. Our soldiers had behaved disgracefully. In fact, the atrocities committed by them on the innocent and defenseless inhabitants of that city were beyond belief. Out of this inferno, two ladies managed to escape. As they tried to flee from the city they were lucky enough to encounter John Kincaid and Harry Smith, two young officers of the 95th. The elder lady explained that she was the wife of a Spanish officer away at the war. Her home had been wrecked by British looters. The ears of both ladies were torn where their earrings had been ripped off. The elder woman was terrified that her young fourteen-year-old sister would fall into the hands of the soldiery, and she appealed to the two officers for help and protection. Kincaid and Smith were by this time smitten by the charms of the young girl—"

"The fourteen-year-old!" exclaimed Isabella.

"Yes. Kincaid is a fine man. Smith is ten years the girl's senior, vain and somewhat self-satisfied, but she appeared to favor him rather than Kincaid. That young Spanish girl is the now famous Juana, Mrs. Harry Smith. The courtship of Harry and Juana lasted only two days. Then they were married. She quickly became the darling of the troops, for she could ride as well as she could sing and dance, and she is always cheerful and laughing. She can ride all day long and then sleep on a bed of damp grass, only to rise in the morning as fresh as the dew. Harry is like a dog with two tails, he is so proud of her. And she adores him."

"But," ventured Isabella, "perhaps this Juana was already used to a rougher life than that of an English lady."

"Fustian. Young Spanish girls have a much stricter upbringing than any English miss. Juana is possessed of a natural gaiety and courage. She is also, as I have said, devoted to her husband and does not cause trouble with flirtations. I detest flirts," added Lord Harry. He turned to the earl. "You must excuse me, Father, but you have strange tastes in cooking, still. Have you not noticed that your guests can barely get through the nauseating mess on their plates?"

"Mind your tongue, you young whippersnapper," roared the earl, noticing his butler sliding from the dining room. "Stokes will tell Fortheringay what you have just said and then we'll have a *scene.* And I can't abide scenes."

"We are really not very hungry," said Mrs. Chadbury, nervously eyeing the door of the dining room.

"You always were a picky child, Harry," commented the countess. "Do not be alarmed, Isabella. I am sure you can train him to appreciate good cooking."

Isabella said nothing. She felt that Lord Harry

had deliberately selected this wretched Juana out of all the women in the Peninsular Wars to make her feel useless and inadequate.

Lord Harry, too, had fallen silent. He was suddenly remembering a brief return to England after the disastrous Battle of Corunna, a visit too short to allow him to go home.

He and some fellow officers were climbing out of the longboat into the sea on the English coast when one of the officer's wives who had been waiting on the shore to greet him had waded into the sea and clasped her husband in her arms, and so they had stood, deaf and blind to everything and everyone, kissing and embracing, holding each other tightly. He remembered how the woman's pretty white muslin dress had risen and fallen on the waves. He remembered their passion. He wondered what it would be like to love and be loved in such a way and felt sad because he had never experienced such emotion and doubted if he ever would.

The door was flung open, and Fortheringay burst in, clutching a meat cleaver, his dingy apron stained with blood. He was a small, gray-haired man with pinkish eyes and matted gray hair poking out beneath a skull cap.

"I cook the best bit o' beef in the whole of the south of England," he howled. "What's this about me producing messes?"

"Nobody criticized your cooking," lied the earl, but the butler who had followed the cook in said gleefully, "Twaur Lord Harry said it, that it waur."

Lord Harry rose and darted behind Captain

James's chair and crouched down on the floor. "Save me," he squeaked.

"Get to your feet, milksop," howled the earl. "Frightened of a servant? Get you gone, Fortheringay. Everyone enjoyed the meal very much."

"They ain't eating it," said the cook, standing his ground. The Chadburys nervously took up knife and fork and tried to force some food down.

But Lucy, burning with shame for the behavior of her foppish brother, rose to her feet. She forgot about her intentions of behaving like a lady. She picked up her uneaten plate of food and hurled it across the room at the cook's head. Fortheringay ducked, and it smashed against the dining room wall.

"Get belowstairs this minute," said Lucy, advancing on the cook and brandishing her table knife.

Fortheringay stubbornly stood his ground until Lucy picked up the claret jug and shied that at his head as well. He nipped out and slammed the door behind him.

"And you, too, Stokes," shouted Lucy, her hand reached for the Madeira decanter.

When the butler had gone, Lucy, very pink, walked round to where her brother was crouched and ordered, "Get back to your seat, Harry. You are a disgrace to your family and a disgrace to the British army. Coward!"

Lord Harry amiably regained his seat. "It was not my person I feared for," he said in a high voice, "but my clothes. Pon rep, I did not want this coat to be slashed by that maniac."

"That maniac," said Lucy evenly, "is only old Fortheringay whom you have known since you were in short coats." She turned to her father. "But the food is disgusting. Have you never noticed that I barely eat at meals? I go to the kitchens when Fortheringay is sleeping off his latest raid on your cellars and make my own meals."

"That will not do you the slightest harm, my dear," said the countess placidly. "All young girls should know how to cook."

Lucy recollected her role and primly regained her seat. James found himself feeling very sorry for her. Some gallant should ride to her rescue and take her away to civilization. He then looked at Isabella. She was peeling an apple and, despite the shabby dress she was wearing, looked as cool and fresh as a spring morning. He wondered whether Harry had been too fast to damn her out of hand as a narcissistic flirt. She had been assaulted, and instead of fainting and screaming, she had borne the experience with remarkable fortitude. She was calmly coping with this horrible dinner very well.

But Mrs. Chadbury, who had been watching her daughter anxiously, said that she felt they should make an early evening of it and take Isabella home. And so they all went outside to wave good-bye to the Chadburys as they were escorted off by a considerable battalion of servants, all armed to the teeth in case Isabella's assailant should try to attack her again. Isabella called from the carriage window, "I shall see you tomorrow, Lucy. The treasure, you know. And I shall bring enough for a picnic."

Captain James fell into step beside Lucy as they turned back into the castle. "You appear very fond of Isabella," he said.

"Yes, I love her very much," replied Lucy simply. She sighed. "But it is a good thing I am not of a jealous nature. I would give anything to be as beautiful as Isabella."

He looked down at the pert, freckled face, the frizzy auburn hair, and the gentle mouth and said, "I would call you endearing, Lady Lucy."

Her eyes flew to meet his, startled, as if seeing him for the first time. "That is a wonderful thing to say," said Lucy. Then her face fell. "But I am sure you are practiced in the art of compliments."

"Not at all, I assure you."

"Does not my brother irritate you with his dreadful clothes and his mincing ways?" asked Lucy curiously.

Remembering they were *his* clothes, the captain said defensively, "I would not describe his clothes as dreadful. In fact, they are of an excellent cut."

"But so tight. Does he go into battle like that?"

"No, he is very brave and is respected by the men."

"I suppose I must believe you. But why cannot he be easy in his dress like you?"

"The Prince Regent spends a great deal of time and money on his dress," said James, ignoring her question.

"Yes, but he is a *prince*! Do you think Harry will come treasure hunting with us tomorrow, or will he be frightened of dirtying his clothes?"

"I am sure he would not miss it for anything. Why? Are we going to be in someplace dirty?"

"Who knows!" said Lucy gaily. "But a real treasure hunt is a very dirtying business indeed."

Chapter Four

ORD HARRY FOUND he could not face another day in tight clothes and so he and James changed their wardrobes back again. If he still painted his face and affected a languid simpering manner, reasoned Lord Harry, that should suffice. The captain was glad to rescue his coats from the stretching they were enduring across Harry's broad shoulders.

James found he was looking forward to the prospect of the treasure hunt. Lord Harry had once described his little sister as a hoyden, but the captain thought Lucy charming and never knew that Lady Lucy had been up at dawn, feverishly examining one gown after the other. For the first time, Lucy felt cross with her parents' eccentricities. There should be at least one woman in the house to help her. She was therefore grateful and relieved when Isabella's correct lady's maid arrived early that morning to offer her services and brought with her some of Isabella's old gowns—in Isabella's case, last year's, the riding dress being the only relic of her past—to pin and alter to fit Lucy's smaller height.

So when the party gathered at eleven o'clock in the morning room, Lucy surprised her parents and brother by appearing in a white morning gown with three flounces at the hem and fastened at the waist with a broad blue silk ribbon. Her frizzy hair had been teased into curls with the tongs and embellished with a blue silk bow to match her sash. Lucy in turn surveyed her brother. She was glad to notice his dress was more . . . sensible, but the white paint on his face had been applied with an inexpert hand, and one little circle of tanned skin was showing on the left cheekbone. Lucy pointed this out and Lord Harry let out a squawk and ran to the mirror and began to repair the damage with finicky fingers while Isabella looked down at her lap to hide the flash of contempt in her eyes.

"If you have quite finished preening," said the earl crossly to his son's back, "perhaps you might care to look at these old plans of the castle."

"I didn't know we had any," said Lucy, pink with excitement as the earl spread them out on the table. They all sat at chairs round the table while Lord Harry, forgetting his act with the quizzing glass, bent over the plans. "I cannot see anything here," he said at last, "that I did not know about before. No priest holes, no dungeons, no forgotten cellars."

"Oh, but there must be!" cried Lucy, and Captain James, who was sitting next to her, sympathetically turned the plans around so that they both could study them. Isabella stood up and leaned over their shoulders. She had tried to mess up her appearance and thought she had succeeded, being unaware that her simple hairstyle of loose curls and her plain gown made her look more beautiful than ever.

"Perhaps in the grounds," murmured Isabella. "It is not on these plans but there is that old folly on the eastern side of the castle."

"Capital place!" said Lucy, clapping her hands. "Let us start immediately."

"Too romantic a place for my father to think of," protested the earl. "He was not a romantic man."

"He must have been romantic if he did not want Mama to have Grandmama's jewels," said Lucy. "He loved Grandmama so much that he thought no one else was worthy of them."

"A pleasant thought," remarked the countess, "but the fact is the old horror hated me on sight. I was monstrous happy when he died, was I not, my precious?"

The earl, thus appealed to, said, "You could have danced on his grave. Of course, he had gone decidedly odd in his cockloft. I think it was your very great beauty that upset him so, my dear."

The countess's raddled face broke into a beatific smile, and she patted her dyed golden hair. "Yes, you always did say I was the only diamond you wanted, so a pox on the old man's treasure."

"But don't you see," said Lucy, jumping up and down on her seat, "if we find all the jewels, then Harry won't have to marry Isabella!"

There was a shocked silence while Lucy blushed fiery red.

"Show me where this folly is," said James, taking pity on Lucy.

"Yes, yes," said Lucy hurriedly. "Come with me, Isabella."

The two girls walked ahead of the men out into the grounds.

"Lucy, ladies never make remarks like that," said Isabella severely.

"I know. I know," said Lucy wretchedly. "My wicked tongue. But it's true, you know."

Isabella sighed. "It may as well be Lord Harry as anyone else, Lucy, for if I turn him down, my parents will find someone else. Your brother has made it quite plain he only wants me for my money and says that after we are married, I may lead my own life."

"How odd!" Lucy glanced back at her brother. "How Harry has changed! I mean, one would think battles and blood would coarsen a man but they seemed to have worked the other way in Harry's case."

"Is it usual to take such a long leave?" asked Isabella.

"Oh, yes." Lucy nodded wisely. "I heard all about it from old Colonel Whitebeam who lives the other side of Dowlas. He says that it is very hard to get leave and so when a man does, he stays away as much as possible. Harry has been at the wars for years, and we could be fighting Napoleon for ages and ages, you know. If it is any consolation to you, Isabella, once Harry goes back, he could be away from you for years and years."

They walked on in silence. Isabella felt a lightening of her heart. It was to be a marriage in name only. She could have fared much worse. Her parents could have arranged a marriage with a lecherous brute. Isabella shuddered. There was nothing to *fear* from Lord Harry, but he was an irritating creature. He could have been extremely handsome, but his face was marred with white paint and his figure by a mincing walk and manner.

The folly had been built about sixty years ago, a picturesque ruin. It had been very fashionable to have a ruin in the eighteenth century.

It had lancet windows and broken columns and ivy growing about it. The path that led to it was overgrown and weedy, the verges thick with Queen Anne's lace and buttercups. The sky above was cerulean blue and the air still and sultry. Beyond the folly, they could see the sea dotted with the brown sails of fishing boats. Lucy tried to open the mock medieval iron-studded oak door of the folly, but it was wedged shut with damp and disuse.

"Now what are we to do?" asked Lucy. "Shall I go and get some of the servants to break it down?"

Lord Harry forgot his role. "Stand back," he ordered. He raised his booted foot and kicked the door hard. With a groaning, protesting noise the door swung open.

Isabella eyed Lord Harry doubtfully. That had been a powerful kick. But he saw her watching him and immediately took a lace-edged handkerchief from his pocket and began to polish his boot carefully, examining the leather for the slightest scratch.

"What an odd sort of place!" Lucy's voice echoed from the dark inside. "Did we ever come here as children, Harry?"

He finished polishing his boot and walked inside with Isabella and the captain.

"I don't think I ever did," he said. "I don't know about you." Sunlight streamed in through the stained glass of a pointed window, turning him into a harlequin. "What a mess. Of course the roof is broken, or rather that is the way it was built, made to look broken, and so the rain has been pouring in here for years and years."

"Well, let's start looking about," said Lucy eagerly.

"There's just this one room," said the captain. "Look at the brickwork. Nothing can be hidden in the walls. Nothing in the structure has been dislodged or moved since it was built."

"But there's a fireplace," pointed out Isabella. "Why a fireplace in a folly?"

"If I remember rightly, Grandpapa employed one of the locals to act as hermit when he had guests," said Lord Harry. "It was fashionable to have a hermit in your ruin. Look, there's an old pewter plate down by the fire. One of the hermit's dishes, no doubt. Come along. There's nothing here."

"But the chimney," protested Lucy. "People sometimes hide things up chimneys. I once hid a box of cigars up mine." She looked at Captain James and colored. "Well, I was very young and wanted to see what smoking one of them was like."

"It is all dirty," said Isabella sharply. "You will get soot on your gown, Lucy."

"Just a look." Lucy approached the fireplace, which was a small version of a large medieval one with the Tremayne coat of arms carved on the stone mantle and two griffins as caryatids. She bent down and peered up the chimney. "It's all black," mourned Lucy, "but there are iron rungs for a sweep's climbing boy." She stepped into the hearth, and her head vanished up the chimney.

"Lucy," screamed Isabella. "Your gown!"

"But there's a ledge a little bit up," came Lucy's hollow-sounding voice. "And . . . and the rest of you are too big to get in here."

So much for trying to turn Lucy into a lady, thought Isabella, as Lucy began to climb up inside the chimney.

"Faugh! That child is a disgrace, stap me if she ain't," drawled Lord Harry.

"She is a very human and very loveable girl," said Isabella. "Not that I would expect such as you to notice such virtues."

"There's something up here," came Lucy's voice, squeaky with excitement. "A box. A metal box. It's very sooty. Oooooh!"

Lucy fell down the chimney with a resounding crash, clutching a small metal box.

Captain James rushed to help her to her feet. She had lost her hair ribbon, and her face and gown were smeared with soot. But her large eyes were shining. "I haven't broken anything," said Lucy. "Let us open this box. What are the jewels like again, Harry? There's those diamonds Grandmama is wearing in the portrait."

"They were supposed to be all diamonds," said Lord Harry, "and a great quantity of them. Unless they were prized from their settings, they would never all go in that small box."

"It's locked," said James. He took out a penknife

and fiddled delicately with the lock. There was a satisfying click, and the box sprang open. "You *are* clever," exclaimed Lucy. "You must teach me how to do that. Oh, dear."

There was nothing in the box but a folded piece of old paper.

"Let's read it anyway," urged Isabella. "It must be something important, else why would someone have gone to the trouble to hide it up in the dirty chimney of this folly?"

"Lucy should have the honor," said Lord Harry. "Go on, pest, tell us what it says."

Lucy began to read it in her high, schoolgirlish voice. " 'Thought it was the Diamonds, did you not? They will Never be found by such an Unintelligent Whore as you. You are the Ruination of my Son and Bad Cess to you. Tremayne.' "

Lucy's face was pink. "That's Grandpapa," she said. "He really did hate Mama, did he not?"

"But it shows the jewels exist," said Isabella. "Lucy, he says they will never be found by such an unintelligent . . . erm . . . as you, which means the note was meant for your mother, but it also means he thinks he has been very clever in hiding them and that only a very clever person will discover their whereabouts."

"Oh, dear. I'm not very clever," said Lucy.

"But you must be. You found a clue," said James, smiling down at her suddenly. Lucy looked up at him, her mouth a little open, and then she looked down at the ruin of that pretty gown.

"We had better return to the castle so that Lucy

may wash and change," said Isabella. "Besides, we are to have a picnic."

"Does that mean bloody beef outside the castle instead of in?" asked Lord Harry.

"No, the cooking has been done by the chef at Appleton House, and Mama and Papa are bringing it over. Are you going to show that letter to your mother, Lucy? It is very cruel, and I do not think it would do her any good to read it."

"Perhaps. But it does show Grandpapa had also thought of places where she might look. Perhaps there were other notes. Perhaps I shall tell her after all."

"But such coarseness," protested Isabella.

"Mama can be quite coarse herself. We shall see."

The picnic was postponed for half an hour so that Lucy should find time to clean and change.

Captain James was amused at the contrast between the two families, the Chadburys and the Tremaynes. He was sure that had the earl and countess been organizing the picnic, they would all have ended up sprawled on the grass and eating quite dreadful food.

But the Chadburys had brought their own servants, and a table had been set up on the shaggy lawn in front of the castle, spread with a white cloth, and then covered with every imaginable delicacy. There was even iced champagne, the Chadburys boasting an icehouse.

Lucy was glad she had allowed Isabella and her lady's maid to get to work on her. She was clean and scented with rose water and this time wearing a pale green muslin gown. For Captain James in a coat of Bath superfine with gold buttons and a white waistcoat looked very remote and elegant and no longer the sort of gentleman with whom she could feel at ease.

"Tremayne and I have been making *plans*," said the countess, easing her white stockinged feet out of her shoes, for the heat of the day had made her feet swell. "Mr. and Mrs. Chadbury have kindly suggested that Lucy should go with them to the Little Season to get used to London ways."

"Oh, that is very kind of you," said Lucy punctiliously, although she felt scared at the prospect. All those rules and regulations of society still to be learned! What if she disgraced herself?

"And," went on the countess, waving her champagne glass so that some of the golden liquid splashed down onto a dish of ortolans, "Tremayne and I have decided to hold a ball, here, in the castle."

"Why?" asked Lord Harry.

"To announce your engagement to the duchy, of course."

"I have tried to persuade Lady Tremayne to use Appleton House," said Mrs. Chadbury.

"Nonsense," said the countess. "We shall have the ball in the great hall."

"Is it big enough?" asked James.

"Vast," said Lord Harry, "but you'd never guess it. It's divided up with so many old dusty screens and set about with bits of rubbish. I suppose if it were cleaned out, it might do very well. When is this ball to be, Mama?"

"A week's time," said the countess. "Impromptu.

I like the impromptu. I am a famously good dancer, am I not, my love?"

"Like a fairy," said the earl sleepily. "But will anyone come at such short notice?"

"Of course they will," said the countess. "Curiosity will bring 'em in droves. How did the treasure hunt go?"

Lucy made up her mind. "We found a rude note from Grandpapa in the chimney of the folly."

"Oh, another note," sighed the countess. "Still calling me the whore of Babylon, is he?"

"Something like that," said Lucy. "You mean there have been other notes?"

"Well, yes, for we did search years ago. Let me see, there was a really nasty one inside a suit of armor in the hall, and a poisonous one in that china vase on the console table in the drawing room, and, um, let me see, one in a chamberpot in the Blue Room in the east wing, the bit that's just fallen over the cliff, and some others but too tedious to relate."

"Don't you see," cried Isabella, "that the diamonds must be somewhere? The attics?"

"No attic in a castle, Isabella. There are nasty little rooms all over the place, I grant you, but I am sure we searched them all. The servants can't have found them, for if they had they would have left us long ago. I think the silly old fool—I am sorry to call your papa a silly old fool, my precious, but he was, very—probably threw them in the sea in a fit of choleric spite. The mermaids are probably swimming about bedecked with gems."

Isabella gave a gurgle of laughter. "What a lovely

71

picture. Shining and glittering in the green depths of the sea. All those mermaids, combing their long hair with jeweled combs and holding up silver mirrors to admire the effect."

Lord Harry looked curiously at his betrothed. Her hazel eyes were sparkling, and the sun was glinting in the thick tresses of her chestnut hair. He felt a faint qualm of unease. What would it be like to be married to such a beauty and not touch her? Then he gave a mental shrug. She was a cold and selfish heartbreaker, and his parents needed the money.

"Lucy, you should not be drinking champagne," he realized his mother was saying.

"I am getting practice for my debut in London," said Lucy. "Besides, it tastes like lemonade and, compared to the ale in the servants hall, is quite mild."

"You shouldn't have been drinking the servants ale," said the countess severely. "They don't like us in their quarters."

"They never saw me. I stole it," said Lucy.

"Oh, that's all right then." The countess lost interest.

"So do we abandon the treasure hunt?" asked James.

"No." Lucy looked decided. "Now that I know about those notes, I refuse to be defeated. After we have finished eating, I think we should look in the castle itself. A lot of the rooms have been locked up for years and never used. The trouble is, it's not really a real castle or we would have torture chambers and interesting things like that. It was built in the seventeenth century, and so it is about as authentic as that folly."

James looked across the lawn at the bulk of the gray castle. Of course it must be relatively young for a castle, he thought. He had assumed that the west and east wings that jutted out on either side had been added later, but they must have been built on when the castle was new, sticking out on either side of the mock medieval bulk like architectural excrescences. It now had a lopsided look, thanks to the disappearance of part of the east wing.

"What of the ancient battle flags in the hall and the suits of armor," he asked. "Are they real?"

"Of course they are," said the earl in surprise. "With the country cluttered up with miserable relics of the past, who would want to make fakes? My ancestor originally lived farther inland and brought all the family rubbish with him into the castle. He designed the castle himself. Great lover of Hamlet. Wanted it to look like Elsinore. I believe he even dressed up like Prince Hamlet in Danish court dress. Lot of totty-headed people in my past. Good thing *we're* all sane, is it not my love?" he appealed to his wife.

The countess yawned and threw a chicken bone over her shoulder to the three ancient dogs who were lying on the grass, survivals of a hunting pack, now too old to do anything but lie around the castle and snore. "Yes, we are a typically ordinary English family," she said. "In fact, quite boring in our ordinariness. A pox on you, you whoreson!" she suddenly shouted, having spied the old retainer, creeping greedily toward the table, his eyes fastened on the delicacies. "Get back to your quarters. You'll get what's left."

"Crumbs from the rich man's table," said the servant bitterly. "That's all I ever gets."

"You're drunk," snapped the countess, and then promptly forgot about him.

Lucy eyed Captain James nervously from under her gold-tipped lashes. She suddenly wished that she did belong to an ordinary and conventional family like the Chadburys. Then she could feel at ease with such a correct man. She had liked him better when his dress had been more informal.

"What are you thinking?" the captain asked suddenly.

Lucy, startled, spoke the truth. "I was thinking that you suddenly seem unapproachable in your fine dress. I should not have said that," she added miserably.

"But you are looking remarkably fine yourself, Lady Lucy," he said gently.

"Am I?" Lucy looked at him in artless delight. "Isabella is helping me to become a lady. This is one of her altered gowns. Her lady's maid is amazing with a needle, for I am short and plump and Isabella is tall and slim. I am so very anxious to be a lady, you know."

James felt a rush of affection for her. She was so touchingly serious. "You do not need to try to become a lady," he said. "You already are."

Happiness bubbled up inside Lucy. She felt elated and breathless.

"I have eaten enough," sighed Isabella. "I shall

not have the energy now to search for any treasure."

Lucy suddenly jumped to her feet. She ran round the table and seized Isabella by the hand. "Let's run," she urged, "like we used to."

Isabella half protested and then rose to her feet. Holding hands she and Lucy ran off across the lawn, skirts fluttering, running like the wind until they finally collapsed onto a hummock of grass, laughing and breathless.

"You are a hoyden," cried Isabella. "I would not have done such a thing except I was so sure your brother would be shocked."

The laughter left Lucy's eyes and died on her lips. "Oh, dear," she said quietly. "And Captain James will be shocked also."

"He knows you are very young and have not yet made your come-out," said Isabella. "He will think nothing of it."

"No, he will not, will he?" Lucy plucked savagely at the turf and tore up a handful of grass.

Isabella looked at her friend in consternation. "Lucy, dear, are you forming a tendre for the captain?"

Lucy rubbed her snub nose with the back of her hand. Then she shrugged. "What nonsense," she said, leaping lightly to her feet. "Let us go back, Isabella, and rouse those lazybones to help us in the search."

Lord Harry through narrowed eyes watched them approach. His sister was trotting along beside the taller Isabella, looking up into her face and saying something, and then Isabella laughed affectionately and put her arm around Lucy's shoulders and gave her a quick hug.

"Not a cold beauty at all," he thought in surprise. "I wonder . . ." He found himself wondering again about that attempted rape. Isabella had appeared shocked and disgusted and frightened but surely any innocent virgin having undergone such an experience would need more time to recover from it. It was as if she had locked the whole thing away somewhere in her mind. Lord Harry could not know that Isabella had thought her assailant had acted liked any man might behave.

Soon Lord Harry, James, Isabella, and Lucy—armed with an ancient ring of keys were wandering through the castle searching the rooms—while out on the lawn, the earl and countess and Mr. and Mrs. Chadbury made leisurely plans for the ball.

Isabella held back from the others a little as they ploughed through dusty rooms full of old furniture, old documents, and old clothes. She was worried about Lucy. Lucy was an innocent. She could not possibly know what men were like. Isabella looked at Captain James. He and Lucy were peering down into the inside of an old vase. He seemed polite and correct, but those men at the posting house would seem thus when in society.

She closed her eyes tightly and prayed that both Lord Harry and James would be recalled to their regiment. And then as she opened them again, she suddenly remembered that there had been a debate in the House of Commons about British officers spending too much time on leave. What if she wrote a letter to, say, *The Times*, pretending to be some retired colonel. She could complain about Lord Harry and Captain James Godolphin. Surely then the regiment would have to recall them. The boldness of this plan made her eyes sparkle and flushed her cheeks with color.

She found Lord Harry was eyeing her curiously and so she turned away and began to search through the drawers of an old desk.

After several hours, they grew weary of the search. "We'll never find them," groaned Lucy, "and we are wasting all this lovely weather."

"We could ride over to Dowlas tomorrow," suggested Lord Harry. "I mean, we could take a carriage. What do you say, James? We could find some decent food at The George."

"Capital," said the captain.

Lucy's eyes shone in the gloom of the room. "I could buy silk ribbons to trim some of my gowns."

Isabella said nothing. She was anxious to return to her own home and write that letter. If both men were recalled, then she would still be betrothed to Lord Harry, but the wedding would be postponed for an indefinite period, during which she would not be expected to marry anyone else and Lucy would be safe.

Isabella almost hoped it would rain so the outing would be put off, for she did not relish the thought of being so long in Lord Harry's company, and she feared that the more Lucy saw of Captain James, then the more likely she was to fall deeply in love with him.

But the sun shone down from a cloudless sky as the party from the castle arrived to collect her. Isabella had deliberately "dressed down," having removed all the flowers and ribbons from a straw hat and the lace and flounces from a muslin gown.

Lucy was wearing one of her old gowns, but she had cleaned and pressed it herself and had borrowed a frivolous straw hat from her mother that had a whole garden of flowers on the crown.

Isabella wrinkled her nose in distaste as she climbed into the open carriage. Lord Harry was so highly scented, he must have poured a whole bottle of perfume over himself.

"Terrible, isn't it?" said Lucy. "Harry, how can you bear to be so scented? I would hate to have to share a closed carriage with you."

"You are a country bumpkin," drawled Lord Harry.

"On the contrary," retorted Captain James, firing up, "she is a sensible young lady, and you stink like a civet cat, Harry."

"Pooh!" was all Lord Harry would say as he urged the team of horses to a faster pace.

Isabella clutched her reticule on her lap. Inside it was that letter to *The Times*. She would find an excuse to leave the others in Dowlas and go and take it to the mail coach office.

She felt a certain amount of relief at having taken some action and was able to enjoy the drive. Dowlas was a quaint, pretty town with rose-bedecked thatched cottages and well-stocked shops.

They stopped at The George for some lemonade, ordered what dishes they wanted for an early dinner, and then decided to walk to the nearest mercers where Lucy could buy her silks. James offered

Lucy his arm, and she glanced up at him shyly and then turned quite pink with pleasure.

Lord Harry noticed that his friend was more relaxed than he had ever seen him. James was soon helping Lucy to choose silks, saying they must match her eyes, and then looking into Lucy's odd no-color eyes and saying she would need to dye ribbons for no mercer could match them. The captain said this all in a teasing bantering voice, and Lord Harry sensed Isabella's disapproval. "Not a bad match for m' sister," Lord Harry observed, studying the pair through that quizzing glass of his, which Isabella was beginning to hate.

"It would be a very bad match," reproved Isabella. "Lucy is much too young. He is thirty or so."

"Same age as I," commented Lord Harry cheerfully. "And look what a lucky lady you are to have secured such a beau as I."

"I did not secure you," said Isabella evenly. "My parents did. Besides it is very vulgar of you to keep praising yourself."

"Who better? I am much more fashionable than Mr. Brummell, am I not?"

"No, you are not," said Isabella roundly. "Mr. Brummell would never dream of smearing his face with paint or pouring scent all over himself."

"Exactly," agreed Lord Harry amiably, "and that is why I am the more fashionable. We gave a ball in Lisbon, and I was wearing my dress uniform with the gold epaulettes and white net breeches, and do you know what Wellington said when he saw me?"

"I cannot imagine."

"He looked at me and said, 'Good God!'"

Isabella snorted with laughter.

"I amuse you?" Lord Harry raised thin eyebrows. "I am also accounted no end of a wit."

"What do you think, Isabella?" called Lucy. "Captain James thinks I should buy pink ribbons, but pink with reddish hair is not the thing."

"Allow me." Lord Harry rudely pushed in front of Isabella. He took the pink ribbons from Lucy's hand and then walked over to a long mirror and held them up against himself, twisting this way and that to admire the effect. Isabella saw two of the mercer's young men turning away to hide smiles and clutched her reticule for comfort. That letter must be sent.

"I shall leave you to your decision. I shall see you all at The George," she said, and she slipped quickly out of the shop before any of the others could protest.

Isabella heaved a sigh of relief when she got outside. She stood for a moment, blinking in the sunlight, for the shop had been dark, and then set off through the crowds to the mail coach office, which was in The Pelican, The George's rival inn. She began to have an uneasy feeling she was being followed.

Several times she stopped and looked back. A few curious faces stared at her, country faces, ordinary faces. She walked on and reached The Pelican and paid for that letter to be sent express.

She walked back toward The George, half laughing at herself for being so nervous that she was imagining someone would want to follow her. What harm could come to her in a town like Dowlas in the middle of a perfect summer's day?

A little gust of wind set her wide straw hat flapping. She stopped and removed the long hat pin from the crown, meaning to pin it back again more firmly. Then an arm was flung about her shoulders. She looked up into a face that seemed to be a mass of red whiskers and then felt something hard pushed against her side. "A gun, Isabella," said a coarse, harsh voice. "Walk quietly with me or I will shoot you dead."

Isabella stood stock still. Afterward, she felt as if she must have been standing there for hours although it only took a few seconds. Fear was choking her, but she felt the hat pin in her hand and jabbed it viciously into that hand that was holding the gun. The man let out a cry and dropped the gun, which fell with a heavy clatter onto the cobbles.

"Help!" screamed Isabella weakly, and then, "Help!" again, very loudly. With an oath the man scooped up his gun and ran off through the crowd, pushing people aside, cannoning into a cart of vegetables and fruit and sending cabbages and oranges and apples spilling out over the road. "He has a gun," shouted Isabella wildly as she was besieged with questions from all sides. Some of the crowd began to scream for the constable, and others set off in pursuit. With a feeling of relief she never thought she could experience at the sight of him, Isabella saw Lord Harry shouldering his way through the crowd.

He put a comforting arm around her waist, and

she leaned gratefully against him. "What happened?" he asked.

"A man . . . a man thrust a gun in my side and ordered me not to make a sound," said Isabella. "I stabbed his hand with my hat pin, and he dropped the gun and that was when I found I could call for help. He ran off that way."

Lord Harry scanned the crowd and then signaled to a tall young man in farm laborer's dress. "Escort this lady to The George. Here's a crown for you." And then Lord Harry ran off in the direction in which Isabella had pointed.

But of Isabella's assailant, there was no sign. Townspeople under the orders of the constable had rapidly set up barriers outside all the roads leading from the town. Everyone was to be stopped and questioned. The local militia then arrived to give help. Isabella was questioned and requestioned. One unfortunate snuff salesman was dragged from his gig outside the town and his red beard was tugged and pulled for Lord Harry had said he thought the villain might prove to be wearing a disguise.

Mr. and Mrs. Chadbury along with an escort of armed servants arrived later in the afternoon, followed by the earl and countess. The wine merchant from Dowlas had ridden over especially to tell them of the assault on Isabella. The one thing that disturbed all of them was that the man had known Isabella, had used her name.

The countess leaned forward and patted Isabella's hand. "You have been amazing brave, my child, to have protected yourself like that and then to be so calm. Someone is out to rape you."

"Aren't they all?" asked Isabella, and then burst into tears.

As the rest patted her and comforted her, Lord Harry sat deep in thought. He was becoming more and more curious about his betrothed. She had shown exceptional courage, but what had she meant by that remark, "Aren't they all?"

Had some man in London tried to assault her? Was that what had turned her into an ice queen? For why was she so upset at the very idea of a romance between James and Lucy? There was quite a disparity in their ages, but James was kind and decent and very rich, indeed.

Isabella had recovered. The countess was saying they would postpone the ball, but Isabella was protesting wearily that if they were going to have a ball to announce the engagement, then better get it over with.

What an odd female, thought Lord Harry. She was beginning to intrigue him more and more.

Chapter Five

CAPTAIN JAMES KEPT away from the activity of preparations in the castle hall during the following week. He could not imagine the earl or his servants being able to prepare any room for a ball. But Lord Harry assured him that a great deal of help had been drafted from around the countryside, and the earl even had temporary female servants scrubbing the floors. Lucy appeared to have been commandeered by her mother into doing all sorts of tasks, and so James found time lying heavy on his hands.

Many of the guests were to stay the night, and bedrooms that had not been used or even opened in years had to be dusted. To Captain James's relief, he learned from the countess as she passed him one day carrying a bowl of flowers and dripping water everywhere, for she had filled it too full, that the Chadburys' chef was to prepare the supper for the ball.

And then the day before the ball, James found Lucy sitting in the morning room with her feet up on another chair, looking exhausted. Her frizzy hair looked as if a comb had not been through it in days, and she had smut on her nose. The elegant captain, nonetheless, hailed her with relief. "I thought I was never going to see you again."

Lucy jumped to her feet, blushing awkwardly and stammering that she was in her old clothes because there was so much to be done. "Have you seen the hall?" she asked. "It is all going to look wonderful."

"No," replied James. "There has been such noise and crashing and to-ing and fro-ing in there that I have been using the side door to leave the castle."

"Come and see, now," urged Lucy.

He followed her out of the morning room and through a long, stone, flagged corridor and eventually into the huge main hall of the castle. He stood blinking in amazement. The floor of the hall was laid with gold and white tiles that gleamed with polish and looked like a huge chess board. Two servants were polishing an enormous chandelier that glinted and shimmered in the faint light streaming through the mullioned windows. High-backed seventeenth-century chairs lined the walls. Mrs. Chadbury was there supervising the draping of gold silk on two of the walls. "Won't we be grand?" said Lucy. "But let us not stand here too long or Mama will find something for me to do. And I must go to see Isabella about my gown. She is remaking one of her ball gowns for me and sent a note over to say I need a fitting."

"If I can have the use of a carriage, I will drive you over," said the captain.

"Oh, just tell someone to bring it round," said Lucy airily. "The gig will do. I will just change my gown, and then I will meet you outside."

Soon both were bowling along the dusty roads under a glaring sun. "A storm coming," said Lucy wisely.

"How can you be so sure?" asked the captain, looking up at the cloudless sky. "We have been enjoying unbroken weather for some time."

"Too hot and glaring and sultry," said Lucy, "and I noticed this morning that the sea was not so blue. The sea always changes color just before a storm. At first we were going to have a marquee erected on the lawn and have the dancing there, but we could not risk it for we get really dreadful storms on this part of the coast."

She unfurled an old parasol and held it over her. James glanced at it in amusement. It was a heavy cumbersome thing with a dangling fringe, probably dating from the days when the parasol replaced the mask as a concealment for ladies.

"I like visiting Isabella," confided Lucy. "Everything in her home is so well organized. And she has the best lemonade you have ever tasted."

Isabella was sitting on the terrace, reading her letter in *The Times* over and over again. She had pretended to be a Colonel Ferguson. She felt guilty and kept telling herself that she had done the right thing.

But when she looked up and saw the castle gig with Lucy and Captain James, her heart sank. Lucy looked so supremely happy.

She rose and thrust the newspaper under the cushion of her chair as the couple approached the terrace. "Will it be too hot for you here, Lucy?" she asked. "We could go indoors."

"This will do beautifully." Lucy sank down into a chair. "The terrace is still in the shade. And lemonade, Isabella, if you please. I have been telling Captain James about your lemonade."

Isabella picked up a little silver bell from the table in front of her and rang it. A correct footman answered its summons promptly, and Isabella ordered a jug of lemonade. This is how it should be, thought Lucy. When I have a home of my own, everything will be just so. No eccentric servants, no horrible old retainers, and I shall have a lady's maid. Then she looked at Isabella's beauty and sighed and rubbed her snub nose in distress. Probably, if she married, she would have to settle for someone who might not be able to afford such luxuries as well-trained servants and lady's maids.

"Tell me, captain," said Isabella after the lemonade had arrived, "do you not miss your regiment?"

"What you mean," said the captain with a grin, "is that with the country still at war, why am I lounging here?"

Isabella colored and disclaimed.

"It does look odd to anyone who is not a soldier," he went on. "But these wars with Napolean could go on for years, and one must take one's rest from battles when one can. And what better rest is there than sitting drinking lemonade on an English summer's day with two pretty ladies? I am weary of the dirt and stench of battle. Do not worry, Lord Harry and I will return to finish our work, but let us enjoy our rest."

Suffering from pangs of guilt, Isabella quickly

changed the subject and asked how the preparations for the ball were going ahead, and Lucy prattled on happily about how the castle was being transformed.

"Talking about being transformed," said Isabella, rising to her feet, "we must leave Captain James for a short time while you try on your gown, Lucy."

After they had left, Captain James stretched out in his seat and looked out over the manicured lawns and gardens of Appleton House. Then after a time, he decided to have some more lemonade and reached forward to pour himself a glass. It was then that he saw the edge of a newspaper sticking out from under the cushion on the chair on which Isabella had been sitting. He eased the newspaper out. It was the day before's edition of *The Times*. The efficient Chadburys must have it sent down from London to Dowlas by mail coach, he thought. It was folded back at the letters page. His eyes flicked over the letters. Three were complaining about the Prince Regent's extravagance, two about the staggeringly high price of bread, and one. . . .

His own name seemed to leap up at him. He read the letter in growing fury and amazement. Whoever had written it must be someone who knew that he and Harry were on leave. And who on earth was this Colonel Ferguson? But the damage was done. Immediately after the ball, he and Harry would have to ride to Portsmouth and try to get to the bottom of this. And they may as well take their traps as well, for after such a letter as this, it was doubtful if they would be allowed to return. He leaned back and closed his eyes and he was back in Spain, hearing the roar of the cannon, the screams of the wounded and dying. He could feel the hot Spanish sun on his head and hear the monotonous screech of the bullock carts as he and his men wound their way across the high sierras.

"Captain James?"

He opened his eyes. Lucy was looking at him anxiously. Behind her was Isabella, her face half averted, for Isabella had seen that he had found the newspaper.

"Read this," said James, handing the newspaper to Lucy.

She read it quickly, her eyes growing rounder. "Oh," she said miserably. "Oh, how dreadful. Who is this Colonel Ferguson?"

"I do not know," said James. He looked sharply at Isabella who was standing there silently. "Did you read this?"

"No, I have not yet seen the newspaper. As a matter of fact I do not read newspapers. Papa must have left it there," said Isabella, and all at once the captain was sure she was lying.

"I'll read it to you," cried Lucy, and did so.

"Well, to be sure, that is very bad," said Isabella, "but you would have had to return sometime, would you not? Besides, there have been complaints recently in the House about officers spending so much time on leave."

"For a lady who does not read newspapers, you appear to be remarkably well informed," snapped the captain.

"You must not be angry with Isabella," said Lucy, flying to her friend's defense. "It is not as if she had anything to do with it. Oh, dear, I could *kill* this Colonel Ferguson."

"If he exists."

"What can you mean?"

"Just that. No military man would write such a letter. A real colonel who felt strongly about the matter and knew our names would write to our commanding officer."

"What will you do?" Isabella's voice was low.

"Why . . . return!" said the captain bitterly.

Lucy sat down beside him, her eyes wide and sad. She realized she had been living in a sunny dream where she and the captain would slowly drift together into something warmer than friendship. A tear rolled down her freckled nose and plopped on her lap.

"Do not cry," said James gently. He took out an impeccable handkerchief, held her face by the chin, and expertly dried her eyes. "Harry and I have survived this long. We lead charmed lives, I assure you. There now, Lady Lucy, your sympathy touches me. We had best return, for Harry must know of this." There was a slight frost in his manner as he bowed to Isabella.

"You are cross with Isabella," said Lucy as they drove off. "Why?"

"Because, my dear, I have very sharp eyesight. When we drove up, Miss Isabella was seated on the terrace with a newspaper in her hands, and yet she now says she never reads them. She does not want to marry Harry and has been forced into it by her parents and your parents. What better way of delaying the marriage!"

"Isabella would never do such a thing," said Lucy stoutly. "Granted you saw her with the newspaper, but she could just have picked it up because her father left it lying there."

"And thrust it under her cushion? In such a well-run household? I believe more normal behavior would have been to ring the bell and hand the paper to a servant."

"I will not believe it." Tears started to Lucy's eyes. "You do not understand. No *lady* would even know enough about the wars or officers on leave to write such a letter. *I* know, but then I am not a very good example of a young lady, but some of my acquaintance do not even know where Spain *is*."

He slowed the gig and looked at her in consternation. "Now, Lady Lucy, I will not have you cry."

Lucy dried her eyes fiercely. "I know you are upset, Captain James, but there are other possibilities."

"Such as?"

"Well, for example, those two attacks on Isabella. Perhaps some beau she spurned is now determined on revenge and wants Harry out of the way."

"I agree that is a possibility, but I am still very sure that—There now, we will put it out of our minds until after the ball. Will you spare me a dance?"

"As many as you want," said Lucy, suddenly happy again.

The captain forced himself to talk of other things for the rest of the way, but as soon as they arrived at the castle, he went in search of Lord Harry. He found him in his room, lying on top of the bed, fully dressed and smoking a cheroot.

"When my normally indolent parents throw themselves into some activity," said Lord Harry, "it is as well to keep clear. You look grim."

Captain James silently handed him the newspaper that he had taken from Isabella and pointed to the letter.

"Interfering old busybody," said Lord Harry, tossing the paper aside.

"You are not furious?"

"Not really, my friend. This masquerade and the company of the fair Isabella are beginning to bore me. It will be a relief to go back."

"But hear this." The captain described how he had seen Isabella reading the newspaper, of her subsequent denials, and of how sure he was that she was lying.

Lord Harry's face darkened. He swung his long legs out of bed and strode to the window. "A cold-hearted bitch, by George," he said bitterly.

"To be fair, your sister has another idea." James outlined Lucy's theory about the rejected lover.

"Tsch!" Lord Harry swung round. "And yet how is it that I still feel Isabella is responsible. Well, we may be doing her an injustice. This Colonel Ferguson may exist. The trouble is with so many Scottish regiments, there is probably more than one Colonel Ferguson. No regiment mentioned, I see, no address, no club."

"It is very terrible if she did do it," said James slowly, "but have you considered that you might be wrong in your estimation of Isabella?"

"How so?"

"She is remote with us, but with Lady Lucy she is all warmth and friendship. And she cannot be such a very prim young lady to wear that carriage dress or to go running with your sister."

"Oh, I feel that is as much part of an act as my behavior. She is trying to look slovenly to give me a disgust of her but does not know how. She wears unembellished hats and gowns but still manages to look like a fashion plate. There may be depths to her, but they are depths I do not wish to plumb, for I feel I would find nothing but low cunning. I shall ride over to Appleton House and study her behavior and see if I think her guilty of that letter. But first I will go to Dowlas. Do you remember when she slipped away from us and then was attacked. But why did she slip away? I shall go to the mail office and simply ask if Miss Isabella Chadbury sent a letter and to whom did she send it. They know me there, and so they will tell me."

"And should that address prove to be *The Times*?"

Lord Harry suddenly laughed. "Then be damned to her! My parents will need to struggle on. I have some prize money for them, and then before the wars are over, I may have more."

"Wait! You have forgot to paint."

"I am not going to die of lead poisoning because of Isabella Chadbury. I shall retain my foppish manner to the last—the last being the announcement at the ball. Instead of the engagement, I shall publicly announce I have changed my mind."

"Cruel!"

"Not half so cruel as bundling two weary warriors back to the battle front."

Isabella was supervising the finishing touches to Lucy's ball gown. "I think that will do famously," she told her lady's maid. "White jaconet with silver thread, vastly pretty."

A footman entered. "Viscount Tregar has called, miss," he said, "and wishes to speak to you privately."

Isabella bit her lip in consternation. Her parents were both at the castle, still helping the earl and countess with advice about the arrangements. "Very well," she said reluctantly. "Where is he?"

"On the terrace, miss."

Isabella gave instructions for Lucy's dress to be folded in tissue paper and taken to the castle and then made her way slowly downstairs. She paused at the French windows leading to the terrace.

Lord Harry was sprawled at his ease. His hair, worn longer than was fashionable, was combed into a simple style, and his face was lightly tanned and free of paint. He did not look at all foppish. He looked very strong and masculine. She moved forward onto the terrace. He saw her and immediately jumped to his feet and swept her a low and elaborate bow.

"My lord, what can I do for you?" asked Isabella. "Pray be seated."

She sat down herself, and he drew up a chair beside her.

Lord Harry had found out at Dowlas that Isabella had posted a letter to *The Times*. All the anger he felt against her did not show on his face. Instead he said lightly, "Because of some criminal fool writing to the newspapers, it appears that James and I must report back to our regiment immediately after the ball."

"How sad," said Isabella in a colorless voice.

"Sadder for James than I," remarked Lord Harry.

"Why?"

"Well, I have been very lucky in the wars, but poor James has had so many escapes from death that I fear this time his luck will run out."

Isabella's hand, holding a fan, tightened on the sticks. "I am sure you jest, my lord."

In a voice she had not heard him use before, he said harshly, "Death is not a jest." Then his voice resumed its usual mincing tone. "Faith, what sort of man can this Colonel Ferguson be? James has parents and sisters and brothers who would grieve sorely over his death. My erratic parents are very fond of me and Lucy—Lucy would break her heart."

In a trembling voice, Isabella whispered, "Monstrous."

"Yes, monstrous, indeed. But why am I plaguing you with such dark thoughts? Young ladies never think of such things. In fact, in my experience, you ladies never think at all. Your function in life is to look pretty." He glanced at her maliciously, waiting for an outburst, but Isabella was white and silent. "Then I must take my leave. I really called to urge you to look your best at the ball, Miss Isabella. I have noted your dress to be a trifle provincial of late." With that, he strode off in the direction of the stables.

Isabella watched him go, watched him mount his horse and ride off, and then she covered her face with her hands and burst into tears.

On the day of the ball, Lucy felt strung up and nervous. In her dreams, she had been dancing with Captain James. But her dreams had a way of turning into nightmares, and in her latest one, the captain had left her side to pay court to a beautiful lady who was not cursed with either freckles or frizzy hair.

Servants seemed to be running hither and thither in a frenzy, and the countess and Mrs. Chadbury were ordering them this way and that.

The day was very hot and still, and then, to Lucy's dismay, black thunderclouds began to pile up in the west. What if a deluge should fall before the guests arrived, turning the roads into muddy rivers, making any journey impossible?

Isabella arrived in midafternoon to find Lucy walking up and down and wringing her hands.

"Whatever is the matter?" cried Isabella. She received an incoherent tirade about the coming storm, about how the ball would never take place, ending with, "And poor Captain James going back to war where he will be *killed*."

Lucy then collapsed into tears and only Isabella's gentle voice reminding her that Captain James would not like any female with swollen red eyes caused her to make an effort to become calm.

"And my maid has brought my jewel case," said Isabella, "and you may take your pick, Lucy."

The volatile Lucy immediately beamed with pleasure and soon the two girls were sitting in Lucy's bedroom going through the contents of Isabella's case. "See," said Isabella, "there is a cunning little tiara of silver thread and pearls and a fine necklace to go with it."

And as Isabella tried the tiara on Lucy's head and Lucy was admiring herself in the mirror, she suddenly noticed the sadness in her friend's eyes.

"I have been so taken up with my own worries," said Lucy, "that I forgot to ask you how you were faring? You look so sad. Is it because Harry is going back to the battle front? Can you have some feeling for him?"

"I do not like to think of any man going to war." Isabella's voice trembled.

"Isabella, I love my brother dearly for all his nonsense. He is not the type to put himself in the way of getting hurt. Besides, I have often noticed that men *enjoy* wars, although one is not supposed to say so, for they are doing it for king and country."

"I cannot understand what your brother is doing in the army anyway," said Isabella wretchedly. "He is the sort of man who would surely fear any activity that would spoil the line of his coat more than the cannon's roar."

"He was not always so," said Lucy. "Besides, we

have little money, so what else could he do? The only alternative is the church. The gentry go to the navy, the aristocracy to the army. It has always been thus. Now we are both sad. Isabella, this is a ball, a great event, and we are both going to be as fine and sparkling as your jewels."

Isabella smiled. "I shall make a great effort, to please you, and to trounce your brother who pointed out that I had been looking sadly provincial!"

The Chadburys and Tremaynes sat down for dinner before the guests were due to arrive. Lord Harry was determined not to appear a coxcomb before his neighbors in the county, and so he looked as strangely remote and elegant in his dress uniform of red coat and gold epaulettes, white waistcoat and white breeches, as did Captain James, also attired in dress uniform. The only sign of Isabella's continuing guilt and distress were light shadows under her large hazel eyes, but she was exquisitely gowned in white muslin decorated with a gold key pattern. Around her neck was a heavy antique gold collar and on her head an intricate headdress of leaves and ears of corn, all made of beaten gold.

Lord Harry looked across at his little sister and thought she looked very fine. Her gown of white silk ornamented with silver thread had been cleverly shaped to flatter her plump figure, and a pearl and silver tiara gave her an air of dignity.

His mother was dressed in scarlet silk. Diamonds shone round her neck, and a large diamond tiara was perched slightly askew on her improbably golden curls. "Fakes," said the countess, noticing her son's glance, "but good fakes."

"Haven't you anything real left?" asked Lucy.

"Not a gem," said the countess cheerfully. "Stokes sold all the genuine stuff over the years."

"You don't need gems to enhance your beauty," said her husband, giving her a fond look, and the countess simpered and flirted her eyes at him over a large fan made of osprey feathers that was so old it looked as if it had the moult.

Mrs. Chadbury was gowned in dove gray trimmed with lilac, and her plump hand flew up to the very fine sapphires she wore about her neck, almost as if to cover them. She was very fond of the countess and often felt guilty that the Chadburys were rich compared with the Tremaynes.

To Isabella's distress, her father began to talk about that letter in *The Times*; The general opinion of the party, with the exception of Isabella who sat in a strained silence, was that this Colonel Ferguson, if he existed, should be horsewhipped.

"What shall I do with this 'ere?" demanded the old retainer, shuffling in with a post bag. "Tripped over it in the hall."

Mrs. Chadbury looked amused. "My dear Sophia," she said to the countess, "don't you read your post?"

"Not if we can help it," remarked the countess. "Nothing but bills."

"Give it here, Biddle," said Lord Harry. He began to take out a pile of letters and then to sift through them. "Not all for you," he said at last. "One for me and one for you, James."

Both men cracked the seals of their letters and read them.

"Good heavens," said Lord Harry, "I've been summoned back to Portsmouth. Sail next week."

"I've got the same," said James.

"Damn that Colonel Ferguson," growled the earl.

Lord Harry opened his mouth to say something, but then closed it and flashed a warning look at James, but James did not see that look and exclaimed, "But this letter was sent a week ago! So we were going to be asked to go back anyway."

Isabella's face became suffused with a delicate pink. "Guilt removed," thought Lord Harry. "Damn James! I think she deserves to suffer."

But the relief Isabella was feeling was very great. If anything happened to either of them, she would not be tormented by guilt for the rest of her life, for they had been ordered back anyway.

The relief grew and grew, and Isabella became quite merry, teasing Lucy on her appearance and saying she would break hearts that night. Lucy replied that she did not see how anyone with freckles could break even one heart, to which Captain James said he had always found freckles entrancing. Lucy's spirits rocketed and infected the whole party.

They finished their dinner, and then all lined up in a smaller hall that led into the great hall to receive the guests. "Oh, no," exclaimed Lucy, looking through the open door. The sky outside was as black as night, and a sudden rumble of thunder heralded the arriving storm.

"I think it will hold off for long enough," said the

captain reassuringly. He turned round and looked into the great hall. It was magnificent. The tiles were highly polished, and huge displays of roses had been placed at strategic points around the room. On a gallery that ran over the hall, the orchestra was tuning up. The huge chandelier, released from its holland covers for the first time in years, he had learned, shone and sparkled amazingly.

Just as the first guests alighted from their carriages, the orchestra struck up a jaunty air. Lucy felt tears of sheer joy coming to her eyes.

Carriage followed carriage, all the guests eager to reach the shelter of the castle before the storm broke.

Faintly from the servants quarters came the sounds of merriment. The Appleton House servants were on duty at the ball, and so the castle servants were having a party.

Isabella found herself wondering inconsequently how it was that the aged servants of Tregar Castle managed to drink so much, day in and day out, and stay alive.

And then one young man who had just walked into the ballroom said loudly to another, "Faith, Lady Lucy has grown into a little charmer, has she not?"

Isabella gave Lucy an impulsive hug and whispered, "There! You see?" and Lord Harry found himself smiling at Isabella with affection and then reminded himself about that cruel letter. Well, he would have his revenge. He planned to jilt her in the most public, the most humiliating way possible.

As the last guest scurried into the castle, there was a great clap of thunder and the storm broke.

Somehow, the crashing rolling storm outside added to the air of gaiety and splendor inside.

"When do you want me to make the announcement, Harry?" asked the earl.

"After the second waltz, which is just before the supper bell," said Lord Harry. "But I shall make the announcement myself, Father."

"As you will, but it will look deuced odd."

Lord Harry felt a qualm of guilt. He all at once realized that he would not only be hurting Isabella but shaming Mr. and Mrs. Chadbury and distressing his own family.

Lucy was swinging between elation and misery: elation when Captain James danced with her, misery when he danced with anyone else.

At last the waltz before supper was announced, and Lord Harry looked about for Isabella who was supposed to dance it with him, but he could not see her anywhere. The great entrance door to the hall had been closed for the evening as the ghests had come in by another entrance. Lord Harry went out into the smaller hall.

Isabella was standing by the open door, looking out over the rain-washed lawn. He went silently to join her. She half turned and saw him. "I was looking at the moon," she said quietly.

The storm was over, and a great round moon was rising in the sky.

"Our dance, I think," said Lord Harry.

102

She gave a little sigh as if reluctant to leave the moon-washed scene, and before he knew what he was doing, he had taken her in his arms and kissed her.

Isabella was too surprised to protest. His lips were firm and warm and very sweet. The kiss was brief, but when he raised his head, he looked down at her with surprise on his face. Then he tucked her arm in his and led her into the ball room and into the slow, dreamy steps of the waltz.

He forgot about that announcement he had to make. The feel of her in his arms, the scent of her hair was playing havoc with his senses.

Isabella correctly followed his steps while all the time her mind raced. She had been kissed. And for the first time. And ... and ... it had been strange but wonderful. She looked up into his tanned face and clear blue eyes. He was dancing beautifully. He was not mincing or parading. For the first time, she realized he was exceptionally handsome. He looked down into her eyes and smiled, a slow caressing smile, and in confusion, she looked above his head to the crystal chandelier that was blazing and sparkling and glittering like ...

"Diamonds!" cried Isabella. "Diamonds!"

"What? Where?" demanded Lord Harry irritably, for he felt she had broken some spell.

Isabella broke away from him and pointed up at the huge chandelier. "Those are diamonds, I swear," she said. "Your grandmother's diamonds. What a wonderful place to hide them."

Lord Harry looked up, his eyes narrowed, and

then he began to laugh. He clutched hold of Isabella, and both stood hugging each other in delight.

Captain James came up with Lucy, demanding to know what was wrong.

"The diamonds," said Lord Harry. "Up there! The chandelier. A king's ransom in diamonds."

Lucy capered with excitement and then threw her arms around Captain James. One by one the other dancers stopped beside them until the ball room was full of people gazing up in amazement at the great glittering chandelier.

The earl called for a ladder and pushing the servants aside, began to climb. The great crystals were just that—plain crystal, but all the smaller tears strung out along the arms of the giant chandelier were diamonds. He broke one off gently like a connoisseur collecting some exotic fruit and slowly backed down the ladder and presented the diamond to his wife with a courtly bow. "For you, my own, my very precious diamond," he said.

Isabella felt sentimental tears coming to her eyes. There was something so very grand about the normally shabby and indolent earl.

"Let the music start again," shouted the earl, "and we will all dance by the light of the Tremayne fortune."

Isabella moved back into Lord Harry's arms, into a dreamy state, looking occasionally up at his face as the diamonds in the chandelier cast prisms of light over the circling dancers.

When the music finished, the earl came up. "What about that announcement, m'boy," he said anxiously. "This," he pointed to the chandelier, "changes things. Saving your presence, Isabella, but you don't need to marry if you'd rather not, Harry. No official announcement has been made."

Lord Harry looked at Isabella. It was, she thought, as if one moment a very attractive, handsome man was looking at her, and the next had been taken over by a mincing fop.

"La, Papa, do not be worried. I will make an announcement."

He said something to a footman, who called to the guests to be silent for Viscount Tregar.

Lord Harry stood up on a chair. Then he placed one hand on his hip and looked down at the guests with an insolent stare.

"You may have heard rumor that I am to wed Miss Isabella Chadbury," he said in that high mincing voice that so grated on Isabella's nerves. "Well, I am, so you may all congratulate her. Miss Chadbury, you must agree, ladies, has stolen the prize."

"And that," commented Lucy to James as he led her into the supper room, "should go down in history as the most ungracious speech any gentleman ever made about a lady."

"Perhaps he is teasing her," protested James.

"In public? In such a way? And he doesn't need to marry her now."

"No," said James slowly, looking back over his shoulder.

Lord Harry was leading Isabella, holding her by the fingertips of one hand, both their hands held high. He was smiling happily. Isabella's face was averted from him.

Well, she deserved all the misery he could give her, thought James savagely as he remembered the letter Isabella had written. He was grateful there were still pretty little girls like Lucy in the world. She would mature and make some man an excellent wife.

Chapter Six

As if in mourning for the departure of Captain James and Lord Harry, the good weather never returned. A gray June moved onto a bleak July where great waves pounded the base of the cliffs below the castle, and the workers, recently hired to shore up and restore what was left of the east wing, kept complaining they could not work in the gales that battered them daily. August was calmer, but unseasonably cold and misty and the only thing to brighten Lucy's days was that she was to go to London for the Little Season with Isabella as a sort of training for her debut.

Lucy wrote regularly to Captain James, or rather Isabella wrote the letters for her, Lucy's being sadly deficient in spelling and grammar. A change had come over Isabella. All those dreams of love and romance that she had firmly put away were creeping back, as if awakened by Lord Harry's kiss. She did not think of *him* romantically. How could she, after that disgraceful speech at the ball? But vague ideas of some hero would occasionally come into her mind with a longing to meet some man, strong and pure and clean, not like those satyrs of the posting house. She worked hard at composing letters for Lucy to send to Captain James, giving little pictures of day-to-day life in Cornwall, of the weather, of the repairs to the castle, of how the Tremayne family were thoroughly enjoying their newfound wealth.

Isabella privately wondered whether the letters would ever reach Captain James, but a letter from him finally arrived for Lucy at the end of August. To Lucy's disappointment, it was very short, but in it he begged her to keep writing to him, saying her letters were a breath of English air.

Both girls were looking forward to going to London. Mrs. Chadbury wanted them to be there ahead of the start of the Season so as "to nurse the ground" for Lucy, that is, to make sure she received enough social invitations. Lucy had lost her fears, for it had been made plain to her that as this was not to be her debut, she need not feel any pressure about finding a husband. And the pressure on young ladies to find a husband was immense. Parents made it all too plain that the expense of a London Season must not be wasted. Any husband was better than none. Even heiresses such as Isabella, who might have been expected to be free from such expectations, were not. Old maid, ape leader, spinster—dreadful names holding the knell of social doom. The failures could be seen visiting spas about England and Europe, thin, nervous women with all their frustrated mother love turned toward animals or extreme religions, for in most cases their brains had never been furnished with enough education to make them mentally self-sufficient. And so all the training of a young girl was toward one end—to please some man: to laugh charmingly, to sew beautifully, to lisp platitudes, to study every little air and grace that might entrap from "killing" glances to a fluttering fan. Then she must be able to play the pianoforte or sing, for the gentleman had to be entertained. And when the goal was finally reached, the husband caught, the heir produced, the once lively girl was left with an empty brain to pass long days in gossip with other empty brains. The reading of novels was frowned on, but for many it was a lifeline.

Isabella had read widely, and that long summer, she introduced Lucy to the pleasures of books of all descriptions. Lucy privately preferred the romances that fueled her dreams of Captain James, while Isabella began to read articles on the rights of women in *The Lady* magazine, which did not encourage her disgust of men, but rather exercised her brain with a number of new ideas. With the threat of finding a husband removed from her because she was betrothed to Lord Harry, who, with luck, might not return for some years, during which time he hopefully would have changed his mind and found someone else, Isabella lost a great deal of her frozen elegance and laughed and giggled with Lucy and planned all sorts of exciting things to do when they reached London.

Lucy, meanwhile, was losing her puppy fat, and her new gowns had to be taken in again, much to her delight.

The great day for departure to London arrived. The Chadburys' traveling coach stopped at the castle to pick up Lucy, who said a tearful farewell to her parents before climbing aboard. The earl and countess planned to join the Chadburys once the Season had begun.

They had only gone a little way when Lucy began to sense a change in Isabella. She talked little, and her eyes once more held that aloof look.

Finally Lucy opened a letter from Captain James that had arrived that morning. She had been saving it up to read at her leisure. She knew it was from the captain because of his seal.

She read it with startled delight. For the captain said that he and Lord Harry had obtained special permission to journey to London to join them for the Little Season, as Lord Harry had declared that he was promised to be married. Lucy looked at Isabella, wide-eyed. "They are coming home," she cried.

"I know," said Isabella bleakly. She did not have to ask who "they" were.

"But . . . but you did not say anything!"

Isabella's parents had fallen asleep.

"I did not think it important enough," she whispered.

"Not important!" Lucy hissed. "Not important! And I have had your help in writing those letters to the captain. Who told you?"

"I received a short letter from your brother only this morning. He told me to prepare myself for marriage. That was his way of putting it."

"And you do not want to marry Harry? But you said that it might work very well, as he promised it would be a marriage in name only."

"Yes, yes," said Isabella impatiently. "I suppose I must go through with it."

Lucy felt crushed. She wanted nothing to spoil her reunion with the captain. But she wished that reunion could take place in Cornwall and not among all the fashionable belles of London.

They stopped for the night at the posting house where Isabella had seen the scandalous bucks hold that party.

Mrs. Chadbury had noticed during the journey how downcast her daughter had become. As she and her husband were dressing for dinner, she said, "I am concerned for our daughter, Mr. Chadbury. She does not want this marriage. I had become used to seeing her bright and cheerful, and I do not like the change."

Mr. Chadbury's face hardened. "It is either Lord Harry or she will remain an old maid."

"But we could have chosen someone else," pleaded Mrs. Chadbury. "Harry has become so effete and is so insulting."

"He is overly nice in his attitudes, I grant you that," said her husband. "But marriage will mellow him. They will settle down."

"But how *can* they settle down?" Mrs. Chadbury poked an errant curl back up under her muslin cap. "From what he wrote to us, I gather he is returning to the wars as soon as the wedding is over. His letter to Isabella was not at all tactful, you know. Nothing of the lover."

"That is at least honest. He doesn't love her any more than she loves him. It is not unusual."

"But not in our case. Never in our case!"

He put an arm around her plump shoulders. "We were lucky. Isabella is not as you or I. There is a coldness there, a lack of warmth and affection. She will not change."

"But she did change—after they left," pleaded Mrs. Chadbury. "She treats Lucy like a sister. She has been happy this summer, and now that happiness has gone."

"It is time she grew up," said Mr. Chadbury harshly. "At least this time in London we will not have to face disappointed suitors. Isabella has brought this on herself."

Isabella, while this was going on, was standing on the balcony outside the door of her room, looking down into the courtyard. A young lady and gentlemen were standing in the courtyard. Her carriage was waiting, but the gentleman seemed loathe to let her go. He was small and sturdy but quite fashionably dressed. The girl was very young with the prettiness of youth. As Isabella watched, he suddenly knelt down in the courtyard and raised the hem of the girl's traveling dress to his lips; she put out a shaky hand and rested it fleetingly on his brown curls. She said something. He rose and stood before her and then, looking quickly around, he seized her in his arms and kissed her.

When they drew apart, both faces were illuminated with love. A stern chaperone came hurrying into the courtyard, nodded to the young man, and she and the girl climbed into the carriage. As the carriage moved out under the arch of the inn, the girl looked back at the young man, her eyes full of tears, then she dropped her glove to the ground.

He ran forward, picked it up, and stood holding it as the carriage disappeared from view. Then he kissed the glove and put it inside his coat, against his heart.

Isabella drew back, strangely moved. There had not only been love between the two, but tenderness and respect. That was the way it should be. That is the way it never could be for her.

Isabella's spirits recovered somewhat in London. Lucy was so excited at the prospect of this mini debut that she constantly had to be reassured about her appearance. Isabella upset her mother by saying she had no interest in what her bride gown looked like, and so Mrs. Chadbury chose a design from the dressmaker and arranged the fittings, hoping against hope that Lord Harry might prove more loverlike on his return.

The wedding was to be a small one, and it was not to take place in church, but in the drawing room of the Chadbury's town house. Lucy was to be bridesmaid and Captain James was to be the brideman. Mrs. Chadbury fretted over the arrangements flanked by a cold, uninterested daughter and a grim, determined husband. More and more, Mrs. Chadbury wished they had never arranged this marriage.

And then to her further distress, Lord Rupert Fitzjohn came to call. Summoning her husband's support, she received him, bracing herself for recriminations. To the Chadburys' delight, he was quiet and courteous and said he had merely called to pay his respects and to apologize for his angry behavior to Isabella.

Isabella came into the drawing room at that moment and stopped short at the sight of Lord Rupert. He rose and bowed before her and said quietly, "Do not look so afraid. I am here to apologize for my harsh words."

"Then I, too, must apologize for my behavior," said Isabella quietly.

"That is over. As you are now safely engaged, may I beg your parents to allow me to take you for a drive? The weather is fine, and I have an open carriage."

Isabella hesitated, but Mrs. Chadbury, happy that Lord Rupert had shown himself to be so gracious, said, "I am sure a breath of air would do Isabella the world of good."

At that moment Lucy came tripping into the room, and Isabella said, "I am sure Lucy would enjoy a breath of air as well, Lord Rupert." She introduced Lucy to Lord Rupert.

There was nothing else Lord Rupert could do in his new gracious role but to take them both. Noticing that Isabella appeared to be very fond of Lady Lucy, he set himself to please, and so a pleasant drive ended with them all having ices at Gunter's and with Lucy wondering why she could not like Lord Rupert when he was trying so very hard to be pleasant.

Lucy had told Lord Rupert that they were going to the playhouse that night. She regretted it later when she saw Lord Rupert that evening in a box opposite, and sure enough, he presented himself in the Chadburys' box at the interval and made Isabella laugh by saying that the play, which was a historical one about Roundheads and Cavaliers, was so tiresome it made him never want to see anyone buckle his swash again.

Oh, he was easy to listen to, he was kind, he was courteous, and he was charming, and Lucy did not like him one little bit. She did not like his thick sensual lips or his brown eyes that gave nothing away.

Lucy was to attend her first London ball at a Lord and Lady Chomley's. She did so hope that Lord Rupert was not going to be there. Lucy tried to tell Isabella of her dislike, but Isabella only looked at her in amazement and said Lord Rupert was behaving like a true gentleman and that there was nothing about him *to* dislike. So Lucy kept her thoughts to herself and prayed nightly for the return of her brother.

But soon the terrors of her very first ball drove all thoughts of Lord Rupert from her mind. She listened carefully to Isabella's schooling. "Now, Lucy, we will go over it again. I shall play the gentleman. Now I take your hand and squeeze it and say, 'Your beauty inflames my senses.' "

Lucy's eyes lit up. "Oh, do you really think someone would say that to *me*?"

"The gentlemen are quite capable of saying anything. To such a warm compliment, you gently but firmly withdraw your hand, turn your eyes away, and then unfurl your fan with a snap—like so—and fan yourself rapidly. Try that. Ye-es, but not so obviously angry. Elegantly cool, I think. Now, 'Your freshness, your youth, Lady Lucy, make all others at this ball look jaded.' What do you do?"

"He has not taken my hand?"

"No, and the compliment is presented in a light airy manner."

"You are funning, sir."

"No, no, this kind of compliment you must learn to take. If the gentleman is old or ill-favored, you say quietly, 'Why, thank you, sir.' If, however, the man is handsome or you have an interest in him, you proceed to flirt. You unfurl your fan slowly and look at him over the top of it with your eyes teasing a little and you say, 'I'faith, sir, you turn a pretty compliment. You obviously have a deal of practice that I lack.' To which he may say, with his hand on his heart, 'But it is not an empty compliment, Lady Lucy. I mean what I say. Your very freshness, like a budding rose, makes stale compliments impossible.' "

"And what do I say to that?" asked Lucy helplessly.

"You lower your fan and drop your eyelashes. You have pretty eyelashes, Lucy. You lower them long enough for him to admire and then you say with a bantering note in your voice, 'I am sure there are much more interesting things to talk about than my poor self, sir. Have you seen the play?' "

"Oh, I don't like this," said Lucy. "Playing games. Why should I put myself out when I am not interested in any of them?"

Isabella sighed. "I hope I have not turned you

into a rebel, Lucy. Any young girl's role in life is to please men. There is no other. To show yourself indifferent to the beasts—I beg your pardon—to the gentlemen, is impolite. Society will feel if that is your attitude, why not stay at home and knit. I played by the rules. I flirted and charmed, and I thought Mama and Papa would be content. But, no. You must, it seems, marry as well. Be thankful, Lucy, that it is still two years before your official come-out. All you have to do is enjoy yourself."

"But how can I enjoy myself if I am constantly to be on the watch, wondering what to say and who to say it to?"

"Practice, Lucy, and then it becomes second nature. Oh, there is the sound of a carriage arriving. Perhaps Lord Rupert is called to take us on a drive." Isabella ran to the window. She returned, saying, "No, only old Mrs. Fanshawe, come to call on Mama."

"And that disappoints you?" demanded Lucy sharply.

"Yes, it does," said Isabella candidly. "Lord Rupert is so friendly and such easy company, and I need have no fear of him for I am engaged to your brother. I see you are about to lecture me, Lucy, and I will not have it."

"I was only going to say that if you encourage the attentions of Lord Rupert for whatever reason when you are engaged to Harry, all you will do is add to your reputation of being a heartless flirt."

"Lucy!"

"Well . . ." Lucy looked miserably at her hands. "I cannot be other than fond of Harry although he has changed. He is my brother."

"I am not doing anything wrong, Lucy," pleaded Isabella. "If my parents see nothing wrong with my going on an occasional drive with Lord Rupert, then why should you? I have only been on one drive with him, and you were present."

"Yes, that is true. I am a bear, Isabella, but there is something about that man I cannot like."

Isabella knew that Lucy would at least be guaranteed some success at the Chomleys' ball. For the news of the finding of the Tremayne diamonds had quickly spread to London, and Lucy was now an heiress. Also, Isabella considered Captain James too old for her friend and hoped Lucy might find someone nearer her own age.

Just before they were to descend to the carriage that was to take them to the ball, Lucy found she was homesick. A noisy gale was rattling through the chimney pots of London and booming along the narrow streets. The sea would be pounding at the cliffs and blowing across the moorland. She missed her parents' undemanding company, and she even missed the creaking inefficiency of the castle servants. But her parents would be arriving soon, and Lucy gave herself a mental shake and realized her homesickness had been brought on by the sound of the wind and by nervousness over this, her first London ball.

A few streets away, Lord Rupert Fitzjohn was receiving last minute words of advice from his elderly roué of an uncle, Mr. Ajax Duvalle. Mr. Duvalle thought that Lord Rupert meant to try to wed the fair Isabella himself, not guessing at the desire for revenge that still burned under his nephew's showy waistcoat. Lord Rupert knew that his uncle in his time had been the darling of the ladies and so had appealed to him for help in attracting Isabella.

"Now I told you before, m'boy," said Mr. Duvalle in a shaky old voice, "that the ladies are easily frightened out of their wits by any show of lust. Tenderness and respect will get them every time. Isabella must feel *safe* with you, then you throw in the odd sad longing glance and risk the odd pressure of the hand for which you immediately apologize. You can stammer in confusion if you like."

"If I got her in my bed, I'd soon change her tune," growled Lord Rupert, and Mr. Duvalle held up his hands—the palms stained pink with cochineal—in horror.

"You don't even *think* such things when you are courting. There are plenty of ladies of the town to inflict your lusts on. Can you shed tears at will?"

"Me, blubber? No!"

"Then use onion juice. The press of a hand, the eyes filled with manly tears, the broken whisper of what might have been—these are your weapons. Your dress is wrong."

"What!"

"That's an ugly, pushy, mushroom sort of waistcoat, m'boy. Vulgar waistcoat never won fair lady. Plain white for evening. Go and change. Trust me. You smell rank. When did you last have a bath?"

"I don't hold with baths."

"Have one now and get your servants to scent the water."

"Damn, I'll be late."

"If the fair Isabella is as frightened of men as we have decided she is, she will be all the more glad to see someone as safe as you when you eventually arrive."

Isabella did mark his absence at the ball and her eyes kept straying to the door. Despite her bad reputation as a cold-hearted flirt, she still had plenty of partners for she was an heiress, and heiresses were never completely snubbed even when they were engaged to be married. Lucy, she noticed, was proving very popular. She was dressed in correct white muslin, but her youth and gaiety were very attractive.

Lucy came up to her at one point and asked Isabella who was taking her into supper. "Oh, someone or other," said Isabella airily, not wanting to tell Lucy that she had kept the supper dance free in the hope that Lord Rupert would arrive. He was so easy and undemanding.

And then when she had just finished a quadrille, Lord Rupert was there, bowing before her and asking hopefully if by any chance she had a dance left free.

"The next one," said Isabella gaily, "and so you may take me to supper."

The dance was a country one, so there was little opportunity for conversation. When they were seated at supper, Lord Rupert asked her in a low voice if she had heard from her fiancé.

Isabella's low-voiced reply that Lord Harry was expected soon startled Lord Rupert. He must work quickly. He turned his head away from her slightly and said in a stifled voice, "If I had not been such a crass fool ... I have grown up since then." He allowed his voice to tremble. "But how serious I am become," he added. "What a way to entertain a beautiful young lady!" He began to tell her some amusing stories of London society supplied to him by his uncle and was pleased when he succeeded in making her laugh. Soon they were talking like old friends. Lucy watched them uneasily and wished that her brother would arrive soon. Isabella was wearing a headdress of white silk flowers. As Lucy watched, Lord Rupert said something and Isabella blushed, although her eyes were sparkling, and then to Lucy's horror, Isabella extracted one silk rose and gave it to Lord Rupert. Perhaps Isabella was only flirting again, thought Lucy feverishly.

Where, oh, where was Harry?

Lord Harry and Captain James had just arrived at Tregar Castle. Lord Harry found his mother supervising her packing. "Oh, there you are," said the countess gaily as if her son had just returned from a ride instead of from the wars. "You are just in time to escort us to London on the morrow. Not that old gown, Nancy, throw it away."

The countess had acquired a lady's maid at last, a weather-beaten old crone who was related to one of the elderly footmen. Lord Harry eyed the shuffling, mumbling old woman with disfavor, but his mother seemed to find nothing amiss. "It is of no use taking piles of old gowns to London, Harry, when I mean to order a whole new wardrobe. What it *is* to be rich! We are not staying with the Chadburys. We have taken a comfortable town house near the Park."

"With London servants?" inquired Lord Harry hopefully.

"Of course not. Would you have us deprive our old servants of a trip to London? I am quite surprised to see you. You were so rude to poor Isabella at our ball that I had quite decided you really meant to cry off."

"Perhaps," said Lord Harry. "But I was not going to throw up the chance of some more leave. Captain James and I have a month, that is all."

"Well, it is now your decision. If you don't want Isabella, I shall quite understand, for I am sure she don't want you."

For some reason this made Lord Harry angry. "How can you be so casual about it all, Mama?" he said crossly. "She will need to break the engagement anyway, not I."

"Oh, she'll break it all right if you tell her you don't want her. Of course poor Sophia will be annoyed, for they will have to coerce some other fellow into wedding the girl."

"If I did not know Isabella Chadbury to be a hardened flirt, then I could find it in my heart to be sorry for her," said Lord Harry.

"Pooh," said his mother. "What a milksop you

are become! The girl has plenty of money. What more does she want?"

"Perhaps a little love?"

"She gets enough of that from her parents. I told Sophia this age, you spoil that child, and you will live to rue the day."

"Perhaps Mrs. Chadbury might think you have ruined Lucy, allowing her to become such a slattern."

"Fustian. Lucy takes after me, and I am as neat and clean as a new pin," said his mother, wrapping a soiled negligee closer about her. "Is Godolphin with you?"

"Yes, James is with me. We are hungry, Mama."

"Then go and find something to eat. All you have to do is ring the bell."

"When did a bell in this castle ever work? The wires have been broken for years."

"Then use your voice. Shout, for heaven's sake."

So Lord Harry went back downstairs to find James and take him to the dining room, collaring the elderly Biddle on the way and demanding food.

Captain James was depressed to find that he would not be enjoying the luxury of the Chadburys' well-run town house but would be staying with the Tremaynes.

"We'll be eating out a lot," said Lord Harry reassuringly as Captain James wrestled with a piece of cold roast beef.

Isabella's beautiful face rose up in Lord Harry's mind. He stared into space, remembering that kiss. But the least he could do was to give her her free-

dom. She did not want him; she did not want anyone. Let her go.

In the jogging carriage the next morning, Captain James took out the last letter he had received
from Lucy and read it again. Somehow, he thought,
not for the first time, he could never remember the
laughing, hoydenish Lucy when he read her letters.
They were intelligent and well informed and somehow a little intimidating. He would have expected
little Lucy to write a more impulsive letter, perhaps, he realized he had been hoping, a more *affec-
tionate* letter. Not that, he persuaded himself, he
was in any danger of falling in love with a green
girl barely out of the schoolroom.

He and Lord Harry had a carriage to themselves, one in a long line of carriages. Everyone
was going to London from Tregar Castle, every
servant, every horse in the stables, every hawk
and hound and even the three old dogs. The earl
had even had a special carriage made for his small
boat. When they passed through the first town, the
populace turned out to cheer them, convinced it
must be a royal party and the elderly retainers
become so excited by all the attention that they
became even drunker and began to sing snatches
of disgraceful songs.

"What's our first social engagement in London?"
asked Captain James.

"Almack's Assembly Rooms—subscription ball,"
replied Lord Harry. "Mama has managed to get us
vouchers."

"Do you think your sister is enjoying herself in London?"

"Bound to," said Lord Harry easily. "She's an heiress now. She'll have no end of partners."

"Yes . . . yes of course she will," said the captain slowly. "I had forgot that."

Chapter Seven

THERE WAS little chance of either Lord Harry or Captain James calling on the Chadburys when they first arrived in London. Space had to be found to kennel the earl's hawks and hounds and store his boat. Asked tetchily by his son where he intended to hunt or sail, his father replied pettishly that he was sure he could hawk in Hyde Park and sail his boat on the Serpentine, and he could surely find a good day's sport with the Berkeley Hunt, which had been known to pursue the fox as far as the walls of Kensington Palace. Then there was the chaos of the town house to put in order and reluctant servants to dragoon into some sort of service.

"Well, that's that," said Lord Harry at last. "I thought we would never settle down."

"So do we call on the Chadburys?" asked Captain James eagerly.

"No hurry," said Lord Harry laconically. "Let's go to Tats first. I have a mind to buy another horse."

So they joined the motley group of aristocrats and small ferrety horse traders at the famous Tattersall's.

"Wait a bit," exclaimed Lord Harry as a horse was being paraded around the ring. "Now where have I seen that fellow before?"

"What? Where?" demanded the captain, looking about.

"That horse. That chestnut mare."

"Bit showy," commented the captain. "You could do better than that."

"I don't want to buy the cursed animal. I . . . I have it! That ruffian who attacked Isabella. I swear that was his mount."

He waited until the trading was over and then approached the auctioneer. "That big showy chestnut," said Lord Harry. "Where did he come from?"

"Exeter squire, name of Biggins. That's the gentleman over there, my lord."

The squire was a small choleric man wearing an old-fashioned wig under an equally old-fashioned tricorne.

To Lord Harry's questions, he said he had bought the horse the previous June from Lord Rupert Fitzjohn.

"June," said Lord Harry meditatively, after thanking the squire. "That was when Isabella was attacked. Now to find out if she knows this Fitzjohn fellow."

The captain brightened. "You mean we are going to call. What about your horse?"

"Another day will do."

But when they arrived at the Chadburys, it was to learn from a somewhat flustered Mrs. Chadbury that Isabella and Lucy were out driving in the Park.

"Alone?" asked Lord Harry.

"With Lord Rupert Fitzjohn."

"Indeed?" Lord Harry's blue eyes narrowed. "Is Lord Rupert one of your daughter's . . . er . . . rejects?"

"Oh, but he is all that is correct," said Mrs. Chadbury eagerly, "and he is well aware that Isabella is affianced to you."

"We happen to be going to the Park ourselves, ain't we, James? No doubt we shall meet."

"Yes, yes," said Mrs. Chadbury nervously. "She will be so glad to see you."

"Why didn't you tell her of your suspicions about this Lord Rupert?" demanded James when they were outside again.

"I would really like to find out more about him first."

They drove to the Park. It was the fashionable hour and despite the freezing cold of the day, there were many open carriages apart from their own, as the whole point of driving in Hyde Park at five in the afternoon was to be seen doing so.

It was Lucy who saw them first and let out a cry of sheer gladness. "It's Harry—Harry and Captain James." Neither Isabella nor Lucy noticed the shuttered look on Lord Rupert's face.

Isabella found her heart was beating quickly. How handsome Lord Harry looked with his bright blue eyes and strong, tanned face. Beside him, Captain James was as beautifully dressed as ever.

Lord Harry had meant to drop the charade, to stop pretending to be a fop, but he did not recognize jealousy, having never suffered much from it before. He deftly stopped his carriage alongside Lord

Rupert's, swept off his hat, and said in a high mincing voice, "How delightful to see you, Miss Chadbury." Up went that quizzing glass and he stared at her carriage dress. "Too fussy and not a good cut," he sighed, dropping his glass. "You really must allow me to choose your clothes when we are married."

Lucy noticed that James looked at Lord Harry in surprise when he heard that remark. She did not know that James was puzzled as to why Lord Harry had suddenly decided to keep up the act of being effeminate when he had as good as said that he would not marry Isabella. Isabella introduced Lord Rupert.

"Charmed," murmured Lord Harry. "But my dear fellow—that waistcoat! Pink pheasants on a red ground. Faith, it hurts my eyes."

For one brief moment, anger flashed in Lord Rupert's eyes, but then some advice of his uncle's sounded in his ears, "Never take up a quarrel with anyone in front of a lady. Remain courteously silent. He will look like a churl, and you will look like a gentleman." And so he turned to Isabella and said quietly, "The day is too cold to stay here for much longer. Allow me to escort you home. But of course you would perhaps rather change carriages and join your fiancé."

"No, no," said Isabella quickly. She flashed a brief smile at Captain James but studiously avoided looking at Lord Harry. "Lucy and I must prepare for Almack's."

"Harry will take me home. Won't you, Harry?" Lucy fairly scrambled down from Lord Rupert's carriage. James jumped down and assisted Lucy into

Lord Harry's carriage. Isabella bowed from the waist as Lord Rupert drove off.

"Oh, I am so glad to see you," said Lucy. "Harry, you cannot possibly want to marry Isabella. I mean, you don't *need* to."

"How can I possibly change my mind?" demanded Lord Harry. "I have ordered my wedding coat. White silk embroidered with seed pearls. Society will swoon with envy."

Lucy looked at her brother and gave a disappointed sigh. "When I saw you driving up, Harry, you looked so *manly*, I hoped that you had changed back to the Harry I used to know."

Once again, Lord Harry found himself on the point of telling Lucy about the masquerade but stopped himself. Lucy was very fond of Isabella and would no doubt tell her.

"So, Lady Lucy," said James, "may I hope for the pleasure of a dance with you this evening?"

"Oh, yes," said Lucy. "So you are to go! I have been very nervous at the prospect because Almack's is such a *difficult* place. I am told there are dowagers there, not to mention the patronesses, who enjoy catching young ladies out in betisses and faux pas. But now that I know you are going, I think I could face anything."

And that, thought Lucy immediately afterward, is not the way Isabella has trained me to be. I am too forward. I should be calm and elegant. But happiness was bubbling up inside her, making her feel breathless. She was sitting between Lord ~~Rupert~~ *Harry* and Captain James, and as the carriage swung round a corner into Piccadilly, James's thigh

130

pressed against her own and she nearly let out an unladylike whimper, caused by combined ecstacy and pain.

James was relieved to find Lucy much the same. He had been a little taken aback by her new slim modish appearance. He felt happy and at ease in her company and found himself saying, "As Harry is no doubt going to escort Isabella to Almack's, I shall escort you."

"I should like that above all things," said Lucy, turning a shining face up to his, her little snub nose pink with excitement.

"Didn't mean to pick up Isabella," drawled Lord Harry. "Need lots and lots of time to prettify myself. See you there."

Lucy's face fell, and the Captain suddenly could not bear to see all that happiness and excitement extinguished. "You may do as you please, Harry," he said, "but for my part I should consider it a very great honor to escort your sister."

All James needs is a push, thought Lord Harry, but how to give him one? People are very contrary, and if you tell them they can't have something, why they immediately start to want it.

So he laughed and said gaily, "My stars, James, it is a good thing I know you to be nearly twice m'sister's age or I should be forced to ask you your intentions. Which would be utterly ridiculous." And he continued to laugh immoderately while his sister flashed him a look of pure hatred and James sat with his thoughts in a turmoil. He knew Harry was putting on this silly effete act in front of Lucy, and yet he felt that last remark had been Harry's way of warning him off and the more he thought about it, the angrier he became.

By the time they reached the Chadburys' town house, nice little charming Lucy had become imbued with all the fascination of forbidden fruit. The captain found himself pressing her little gloved hand very warmly when he said good-bye, and Lucy responded naturally in a way that would have pleased Isabella could she have seen it. Down came those ridiculously long lashes over pink cheeks and very slightly the pressure of his hand was returned.

She went straight up to her bedchamber to begin the long preparations for the ball, unaware that Isabella was at that moment entertaining Lord Rupert.

"I should not be alone with you," Isabella was saying. "I invited you because I thought my mother would be present."

"I will only stay a moment," he said. "With your fiancé returned to you, Miss Chadbury, I cannot indulge myself further in these visits."

Isabella slightly turned her head away. "No," she agreed mournfully. "It would not be correct."

"But perhaps you may grant me one dance this evening?"

"Certainly, my lord."

He rose and bowed and then crossed to the door, where he stood for a few moments with his back to her. Then he swung about and said to her seriously, "But I would have you know that you may turn to me if you are in any trouble. I will always be there."

He had the satisfaction of seeing tears shine in

Isabella's large eyes. He knew his guess had been right. She did not want to marry Lord Harry.

"Thank you," she said in a stiffled voice. He bowed again and left.

"So these are the facts as we know them," Lord Harry was saying. "Lord Rupert Fitzjohn sold a horse to the squire in Exeter. He could have fled to Exeter on his way back to London after trying to assault Isabella. He could have realized that the horse might mark him, and so he got rid of it. He has been rejected by Isabella. Now he may simply be a man crazed with passion. On the other hand, he may be extremely vain, vain to the point of madness. I know I was acting the fop, but did you see that waistcoat of his? Only a madman would sport something like that in the Park."

"Now you sound like the fop you pretend to be," said James acidly.

"What's given you the blue devils?"

"I do not like being made to feel an old man in front of your sister!"

"You are too sensitive. Did I call you an old man? Of course not. I merely stated a fact and that fact is that you are nearly twice my sister's age."

"I am thirty. Your sister is nearly eighteen. Isabella is nineteen and yet that does not seem to faze you. I fear your act is taking over and becoming the reality, Harry. You are in danger of becoming a posturing fool. It should have been your concern to escort your sister to her first evening at Almack's."

"Lucy is well able to look after herself," said Lord Harry, deliberately appearing to stifle a yawn.

"Well, I am going to bathe and change and leave you to your meditations. But consider this. Your behavior to Isabella will be enough to drive her into the arms of any man other than you."

The captain stalked out. Lord Harry swung his feet up on a chair opposite and thoughtfully studied his distorted face reflected in the shiny toecaps of his boots. He would need to watch Lord Rupert closely, perhaps get to know him. If the man were genuine in his love for Isabella, then he could have her. But Lord Harry's face suddenly darkened. Damn him! No man who prowled the countryside waiting to assault a female to exact revenge was trustworthy. No passion on this earth could excuse such behavior. To warn Isabella, he shrewdly guessed, would be to drive her further into Lord Rupert's hairy arms. "And I am sure he does have hairy arms," said Lord Harry aloud and viciously, causing one of the tottering old servants who had come in to make up the fire to drop the coal scuttle.

Lord Harry had meant, had really intended, to escort Isabella and his sister, but he worried over the problem of Lord Rupert and Isabella until a banging of the street door and a glance at the clock told him the hour was late and James had left without him.

A shadow crossed Lucy's golden evening on the way to the ball when the captain said, "I must thank you for your beautiful letters." Lucy gave him a stricken look and the captain wondered what on earth he had said to upset her. He felt he could not pursue the matter with Isabella and her parents present and wished them all at the devil.

To his relief, Isabella and her parents were hailed by friends, and so he brought Lucy a glass of lemonade and, by turning his back on the Chadburys and shielding her from their view, managed to ask her why she had appeared so distressed when he had mentioned her letters. "I feel like a fraud," said Lucy. "My spelling despite Isabella's schooling this past summer is still atrocious, and so I got Isabella to write them for me. I thought you liked them. You wrote and said they were like a breath of English air."

"I meant a breath of cold English air," said the captain smiling down at her. "I would rather have had your misspelled letters than Miss Chadbury's formal epistles. Now I know she wrote them, I can find it in my heart to feel slightly sorry for your reprehensible brother."

"Do not misjudge Isabella," said Lucy, flying to her friend's defense. "It is very hard surely for someone else to write one's letters. They cannot possibly say the things one wants to say."

His gray eyes teased her. "And can you tell me now what you would have said?"

Lucy looked down at her fan. "Oh, lots of things but . . . but I forget what they were."

"But you remembered me," he said softly, "and that was terribly important."

"I was worried about you," said Lucy in a low voice. "I feared you might have been killed."

135

A young man appeared at Lucy's side and begged the next dance and she curtsied to the captain and walked off with her partner.

James felt a pang of pure jealousy as he watched them go. Did Lucy really need to smile so charmingly up at her partner?

He folded his arms and stood behind the roped enclosure of the ball room floor, determined to secure her for the next dance.

Isabella, he noticed, was dancing gracefully with Lord Rupert Fitzjohn. Where, oh, where was Harry?

Lord Harry made a late and sensational arrival with his parents. But it was not Lord Harry who made the social crowd stop and gasp, but his mother, the countess. Her curls were even brassier than ever, and she was wearing a flame-colored silk gown. Around her neck blazed a diamond necklace and a diamond tiara adorned her hair. There was a diamond brooch on her shoulder and her gown was fastened down the front with diamond clasps. The earl had obviously had a considerable amount of the gems that had hung for so long from the chandelier in his hall set in gold for his wife. The countess preened as she turned this way and that, enjoying the sensation she was creating.

Isabella saw Lord Harry arrive and for a moment was surprised. He was correctly and fashionably dressed in a black evening coat and black silk breeches and white stockings with gold clocks. His blue eyes were dancing with mischief as they ranged around the ball room. It was, reflected

Isabella, like looking at an attractive stranger. And then he saw her and his face changed and became set in lines of pouting discontent. He minced toward her. "I think we should dance," he said, "I believe it is the waltz and I waltz divinely."

"You are come too late," said Isabella in a thin voice. "I did not expect you and therefore have no dances to spare. The waltz is promised to Lord Rupert here."

"Ah, but as you are betrothed to me, I am sure Lord Rupert will gladly give up his dance to me."

Lord Rupert bowed. "It will be my pleasure," he said smoothly and had the satisfaction of seeing the look of annoyance mixed with disdain that flashed in Isabella's eyes.

Lord Harry had quite decided to stop all the nonsense and tell Isabella that he was releasing her from the engagement. But as he put one hand on her pliant waist and took her other hand in his, he experienced a sharp feeling of desire, and that made him very angry indeed. The fact that he had given her every reason to despise him was forgotten. How dare she avert her head from him. Lord Rupert was standing at the edge of the ball room floor watching them as Isabella suddenly looked at him and gave him a rueful smile. Lord Harry saw that smile and tightened his grip on her.

"I cannot wait until we are wed," he murmured. "OH, GOOD HEAVENS!"

His voice had ended on a shriek. He released Isabella, ran to the side of the floor, vaulted the rope, and stood up on a chair and shouted, "A mouse! A mouse!"

Soon the dance floor was in chaos as the ladies rushed hither and thither, holding their skirts tightly around their ankles because everyone knew, although no one really talked about it except occasionally in whispers, that mice had a nasty habit of going *up there*.

Only Isabella, who had no fear of mice, stood stock still where he had left her, her cheeks flaming with embarrassment. "What a milksop Tregar is," said one man to another.

Lord Rupert approached Isabella and smiled down into her eyes. "I think I shall claim my dance after all," he said and led her smoothly in the steps of the waltz.

Isabella looked across at Lord Harry. He was now seated and had produced a small fan from his pocket and was fanning himself languidly while an anxious dowager handed him a glass of water.

"You must not be so distressed," murmured Lord Rupert. "Many are afraid of mice."

"Soldiers?" demanded Isabella contemptuously. "Only silly misses are afraid of mice. Lord Harry was the only man in the ball room to be so afraid."

"There is nothing like the love of a good woman to stiffen a man's spine," he teased. "He will change once you are married."

She wanted to say that she would do anything not to be married to Lord Harry, but convention kept her silent. Lord Rupert wanted her to talk about her fiancé, to reveal something, so that he might have an opportunity to say he would help her. It was all part of his plan of revenge.

They were just leaving the floor when Isabella heard one man say to the other, "Disgraceful exhibition. And in Almack's, too! Did you ever see such a man milliner as Tregar?"

"I shall fetch you some lemonade," said Lord Rupert in a soothing voice. Isabella nodded her head, her thoughts racing. Marriage to Lord Harry would not be a placid arrangement. She doubted very much now whether he was really going to stay in the army. His family had enough money now. He could sell out, and then he would be with her all the time, chattering and preening and humiliating her on every occasion. Tears shone in her large eyes, tears that Lord Rupert noticed immediately he returned with her lemonade. He pasted a look of concern on his face for he was in fact delighted at this sign of distress. She deserved it. Let the galled jade wince!

"Miss Chadbury," his voice was low and soft, "I cannot bear to see your tears. You do not need to tell me. This proposed marriage is repugnant to you. But you do not need to go through with it. I will help you."

"How can you, my lord?" asked Isabella in a stifled voice. "My parents have arranged the marriage with his parents. Neither side will allow me to cry off."

"Is it possible you could meet me tomorrow?" he whispered. "I assure you, I can save you from this."

Too overcome with gratitude at his seeming kindness, Isabella forgot the conventions and looked at him with some hope in her eyes. "I . . . I could perhaps slip away early when all are asleep."

"Go for an early morning ride in the Park," he urged. "Ten o'clock, say." Ten o'clock *was* very early for society.

Isabella saw her next partner approaching and nodded. As she moved off into the set of the next dance, she heard sounds of raucous laughter of a kind never before heard at Almack's. Lord Harry was surrounded by gentlemen. He seemed to be reciting some poetry, lewd to judge from the expressions on the faces around him and by that vulgar laughter. Isabella shivered despite the heat of the ball room. She wondered what Lucy thought of her brother now.

But Lucy had not noticed her brother's behavior. She had eyes only for Captain James. She had even forgotten seeing Isabella give Lord Rupert that flower. She could not even enjoy her own popularity for it meant she could have only two dances with the captain and then suffer other escorts to lead her to the floor. Made selfish by love, she merely thought Isabella a poor sort of creature when, on the road home, Isabella said she had not enjoyed herself at all. For the captain was escorting them home, Lord Harry having gone off to a gambling club with other friends.

Again on leaving, the captain pressed Lucy's hand warmly, and Lucy returned the pressure. Then James raised her hand to his lips. Isabella, wrapped in her own misery, went on into the house, the only little light in her darkness being the prospect of seeing Lord Rupert and finding out how he could help her.

Mr. and Mrs. Chadbury might have been expected to sympathize with their daughter's predicament at Almack's. But Mr. Chadbury had been approached by several of Isabella's rejected suitors who had slyly congratulated him on finding "such a fine fellow" for his daughter and all that had served to do was to remind him of Isabella's "wanton" behavior, as he called it. For her part, Mrs. Chadbury was wavering between trying once more to beg her husband to allow Isabella to break the engagement and yet dreading the thought of having an unmarried daughter on her hands. Having an unmarried daughter was a terrible thing. Besides, Mr. and Mrs. Chadbury were plagued by feelings of guilt, feelings that they had spoiled their daughter and that to give in to her once more, to allow her to reject Lord Harry, would only serve to damage her character further. They therefore persuaded themselves that Lord Harry would come about, that marriage would strengthen his character.

The Earl and Countess of Tremayne were, as usual, too wrapped up in their own affairs. If Harry wanted to go ahead with the marriage, so be it. If he wanted to hop around Almack's, screaming about mice and making a cake of himself, then that was his affair.

Lucy awoke fairly early with a pleasurable feeling of anticipation. Captain James had danced with her, and therefore the conventions demanded that

141

he should call on her this day to present his compliments. Of course, he could always send a servant, also equally correct, but she was happily sure he would not do that.

Isabella's room was next to her own. She could hear Isabella moving about, the sound of splashing water as she washed herself.

Lucy climbed down from her high bed and began to dress as well. It would be fun to talk to Isabella about the ball, by which Lucy meant she wanted to talk to someone, anyone, about the glory that was Captain James Godolphin.

She had just finished dressing when she heard Isabella's bedroom door open and close and then Isabella's light rapid footsteps descending the staircase.

Lucy darted from her room in pursuit and was just in time to see the street door slam. Isabella had gone out!

Lucy ran back upstairs and put on a warm cloak and bonnet and set out herself, wondering where Isabella had gone.

As she stood outside the Chadburys' town house, looking this way and that, she heard a clatter of hooves, and then saw Isabella ride out under the arch that led from the mews at the back.

She did not see Lucy but rode off round the square and disappeared from view.

Without stopping to think, Lucy hurried after her. Frost glittered on the cobbles, and the day was smoky and gray with a small red sun trying to struggle through the pall of smoke that always hung over London.

Lucy headed for Hyde Park. That was where Isabella had surely gone. She still did not think that Isabella had gone to meet anyone, merely that it was odd of her to ride out so early, and, besides, Lucy was eager to talk about her captain.

She skirted the high wall of Hyde Park and entered by the lodge gate that led to Rotten Row.

The first thing she saw was Isabella and Lord Rupert. They were standing beside their horses at the edge of the Row, talking seriously. Puzzled, Lucy began to steal up on them, using the trees as cover.

If Isabella and Lord Rupert had not been so intent on their conversation, then they would certainly have noticed the little figure of Lucy darting from tree to tree.

"I am breaking the bounds of convention," Isabella was saying, "by talking to you about my fiancé, but I am in despair. I do not want this marriage."

His heart exulted. How easy all this was turning out to be.

Isabella then stood silently before him, her head bowed. Behind them a waterfowl squawked, then rose with a great beating of wings into the still and frosty air.

"I said I would help," said Lord Rupert at last. "There is but one way I can help you."

Isabella's beautiful eyes flew to meet his. "Oh, my lord, if only you can think of something, anything."

"Marry me. Elope with me."

Isabella closed her eyes. Oh, that vision of those

writing bodies on the floor of the post house dining room. She turned pale.

"What is it?" he demanded anxiously.

"I must tell you, sir, that I fear the intimacies of marriage."

"As does any gently reared lady," he said while the lecher inside him admired the quick rise and fall of her bosom.

"I was, several years ago, witness to a party held by some bloods and their Cyprians in the posting house. What I saw then disgusted me, appalled me."

He raised her hand to his lips. "And you think I would behave thus to a lady I love and respect! Yes, love, Miss Chadbury. We are not all thus. I promise you,"—he put his hand on his heart—"there would be no intimacy between us until we had been married several years and had come to know each other better. You have had a dreadful experience, but it will soon fade from your mind. I would be your squire, your faithful companion, nothing more. Just say the word, and I can have my traveling carriage waiting at the corner of the square to whirl you away to Scotland. Do you think your parents will not come about? Of course they will. I am rich and titled."

A little distance away, Lucy strained her ears but could not hear a word.

Isabella put her hand to her brow. "Give me time to think."

"I will be at the opera tonight," he said. "All you have to do is nod your head in my direction. At five in the morning, I will have my carriage waiting in the square. Bring only what you need for the journey."

"Oh, this is all so underhand," said Isabella wretchedly. "My lord, give me some time, I beg of you."

"I will wait forever, if necessary," he said in a low voice.

"Until this evening." Isabella swung herself lightly up into the saddle and rode off.

Lucy stayed where she was. She saw the look of solemn respect leave Lord Rupert's face as he watched Isabella go and saw it replaced with a look of triumphant cunning.

Lucy did not know what to do. Isabella should not have been holding assignations with another man while she was betrothed to Harry. She decided the sensible thing would be to return home and ask Isabella outright why she was behaving in such a way. She hurried back and went straight up to Isabella's bedchamber where that lady was just removing her bonnet.

"I followed you," said Lucy breathlessly. "To the Park."

"Why did you do that," asked Isabella evenly, "and why did you not approach me?"

"You were talking to Lord Rupert when I arrived, and so I did not want to interrupt."

"You preferred to spy on me, is that it?"

"But Isabella, it was most odd. Why should you be talking to Lord Rupert so early in the day and without a maid or groom with you?"

Lucy noticed a shade of relief in Isabella's eyes.

Isabella had correctly judged that Lucy had not been able to hear anything.

"I decided to go for an early ride," said Isabella. "Lord Rupert was there by chance. We exchanged a few pleasantries, that is all."

"It looked to me like an assignation," said Lucy.

"You are too romantical, Lucy. Have I not warned you about the pernicious effect of reading too much fiction? Have you ever known me to be other than correct?"

"No-o."

"Well, then, you played spy for nothing, and your little nose is quite red with the cold. Let us go down and find some breakfast."

"I think I will go back to bed," said Lucy huffily, for she was sure Isabella was lying.

Lucy returned to her own room and sat down in a chair by the window with an angry thump. Something was going on. If she spoke to the Chadburys, Isabella would never forgive her. Whom to ask? Then she thought of Captain James and felt a warm glow. She would not admit to herself that this was a perfectly splendid excuse to call on him. Besides, Captain James was living with her parents, so everyone would think she was calling on them.

When she reached her parents' town house, she had to step over the elderly retainer, Biddle, who was lying dead drunk at the foot of the stairs. Stokes, the butler, had said that the captain was in the morning room.

Captain James, who had been reading the newspapers, struggled to his feet as Lucy tripped in. He was wrapped in an elaborate dressing gown. "Forgive my undress, Lady Lucy," he said, "but I did not expect any callers."

Lucy crossed the room and stood on tiptoe to study her face in the glass over the fireplace. "My nose is not red," she said triumphantly. "She only said that because she was nonplussed!"

"Who? What? Sit down, my dear. You look most charming."

Lucy flushed with pleasure and sat down next to him at the table.

"I need your help," she said. "I followed Isabella this morning, and she met Lord Rupert in the Park. She told me it was by chance, but they were talking seriously and in low voices, and he was making love to her with his eyes. And when she left, he looked after her with *such* a nasty expression on his face."

James poured her a cup of coffee and then said, "Begin at the beginning and tell me all."

So Lucy told him every detail, all the while savouring the intimacy of their situation, he in his dressing gown, the clocks ticking, the fire crackling and the coffeepot hissing on the spirit stove.

He looked at her seriously when she had finished, then appeared to make up his mind. "I am going to break a confidence," he said. "Your brother has a mischievous streak. He has been posing as the worst of fops to give Miss Chadbury a disgust of him. He says he has no intention of marrying her, and yet for some reason his behavior gets worse and he will not break it off." He told Lucy about

Lord Rupert's horse ending with, "From what I have told you, Lord Rupert wants revenge on her. But if I tell Harry, he will tax her with it, and she will not believe him. I don't think now she would believe any of us."

"If it is this engagement that is driving her into Lord Rupert's arms," said Lucy, "then all Harry has to do is to tell her of the game he has been playing."

"She would be furious, I think," said the captain. "Don't you?"

"I suppose so," said Lucy, downcast. "Love should be so simple."

"And what do you know of love, my child?"

She looked at him solemnly, her eyes wide.

He leaned forward and kissed her gently on the lips. Lucy mumbled something against his mouth. Startled at his own behavior, he was about to draw back, but two little arms clasped him tightly around the neck and drew him closer. And then it seemed easier to move her onto his lap where he could kiss her more comfortably, a long deep kiss that left them both trembling.

"Lucy, will you marry me?"

"Yes, kiss me again."

"Child, I am so much older than you."

"Too old for kisses?"

"Oh, no, my heart's desire." He kissed her snub nose, her throat, her ears, and her mouth again.

"Very soon," he whispered at last against her mouth. "We must be married before I leave."

Lucy drew back a little and looked at him seriously. "Yes, so that I may come with you."

"You cannot! It would be a hell on earth. The filth, the wounded, the long marches . . ."

She laid a finger on his lips to silence him. "I am going with you," she said.

"I must speak to your parents."

"Come now," said Lucy. He kissed her at the door of the morning room and then on the landing outside and then with a laugh, he swept her up in his arms and kissed her all the way to her parents' bedroom before setting her down outside the door.

"What if they are asleep?" he whispered.

"Then we will go away." Lucy opened the door.

Her parents were both sitting up in bed drinking hot chocolate. Two of the old dogs lay at the foot of the bed snoring loudly, while another lay on the hearth.

The room smelled strongly of unwashed bodies, essence of old dog, woodsmoke, and heavy perfume. The earl and countess thought washing all over one of those irritating new fads.

"I am come," said the captain, "to ask you for your daughter's hand in marriage."

"Lucy?" The countess looked surprised. "Well, if you must, you must. But go away. We do not like to be disturbed so early, do we, my sweet?"

"If you are to be part of this family, you must stop bouncing in and out of people's bedrooms at this unearthly hour," said the earl. "It's only noon. Go away."

"We are getting married very soon," said Lucy.

"Why?" asked the countess curiously. "Not got his leg over you already, has he?"

Shocked and red-faced, the captain pulled Lucy from the room.

"Really!" he said, exasperated, "I thought it odd that your own mother should not supervise your social visit to London, but I declare you are better off with the Chadburys."

"Mama was always rather coarse in her speech," said Lucy. "I had forgot about Harry. What do we tell him?"

"Tell me what?" demanded Lord Harry's voice from behind them.

"First," said James, "that we are to be married, and I do not want any remarks about my age."

"Congratulations, dear boy."

"You mean you do not object?"

"I? Of course not. What a devilish dull evening that was at Almack's. But I did well, did I not? Stirred the place up a bit. I hate Almack's with all its rules and tepid lemonade and old sandwiches. Why do you both stare at me so? Have I not given you both my blessing?"

"You had best come down to the morning room," said the captain quietly. "There is something you should know."

Once in the morning room, they told Lord Harry about Isabella's assignation. "And you have only yourself to blame, Harry," said his sister. "Carrying on like the veriest coxcomb. It is enough to give anyone a disgust of you. And it is of no use lecturing Isabella about this and telling her I have told you, for it will only annoy her the more."

He shrugged. "Lord Rupert is welcome to her."

"But I do not think he loves her!" cried Lucy. "I think he wants revenge."

Lord Harry stood up. "Perhaps I will call on my beloved."

"Do that," said Lucy, "and tell her you don't want to marry her!"

Chapter Eight

$\mathcal{L}$ORD HARRY WENT thoughtfully on his way. He was shrewd enough to know that Isabella would not listen to any warning about Lord Rupert Fitzjohn. But he would call on her first and then see if he could find out what Lord Rupert was planning.

The Chadburys received him with warmth to make up for their private doubts about this prospective son-in-law. Isabella was summoned and at last came reluctantly into the drawing room. She was wearing a morning gown of fine white lace, beautifully cut, and her thick hair was dressed in a simple style. She curtsied to Lord Harry and then sat down on a sofa beside her mother.

Mrs. Chadbury thought Lord Harry was looking more—well—*hopeful* a prospect as a son-in-law than he had done before. He no longer used paint. His well-cut clothes sat easily on his athletic frame, and his blue eyes were serious.

"I am sure, Mr. Chadbury," she said, rising to her feet, "that we can spare Isabella and Lord Harry a few moments alone together."

Mr. Chadbury bowed to Lord Harry and followed his wife from the room. There was a long silence.

The fire crackled, the clocks ticked, but Isabella felt none of that cozy intimacy so recently enjoyed with Lucy. Outside a hawker shouted his wares, and a carriage clattered over the cobbles.

So here we sit, thought Lord Harry, two members of society bound by the conventions. She wants to scream, I hate you, and I? . . . I should be telling her that it was all a game and that she is free. His conscience suddenly nagged him. That beautiful face across from his was made for love and laughter. But not for Lord Rupert's kisses, he thought savagely.

"We do not appear to be very suited," he said at last.

Her hazel eyes filled with hope and she said, "No, indeed, you would be happier with anyone else, I think."

She moved slightly and carefully arranged the drapery of her gown. He had a sudden fierce longing to clasp her in his arms and was alarmed at the intensity of his feelings. He began to grow angry. "But we are engaged," he remarked in a neutral voice, "and so must make the best of it."

The light died out of those eyes. She pleated a fold of her gown with nervous fingers. "You do not need to marry me now," she said. "You are rich. My money *was* the attraction, you must admit."

"It was . . . but not now."

"What then, pray?"

"Your face, your figure, your love."

Startled, she gazed at him. He was no longer the fop. He looked strong and masculine and seemed to exude a mixture of sensuality and predatory maleness. She shuddered and dropped her eyes.

"And so, Isabella, my love, you are going to have to make the best of it."

In her mind's eye rose a picture of Lord Rupert's face. All she had to do was to nod to him at the opera, and then she would be free.

He rose to his feet and stood looking down at her. "I shall be here this evening to escort you to the opera." He rose and stalked from the room.

Tears welled up in Isabella's eyes and slowly rolled down her cheeks. Mrs. Chadbury, entering the room, saw those tears. She turned to her husband who was behind her and said severely, "We must talk." She led him away and into a little used ante room and faced him. "I have been your dutiful and obedient wife these many years, but I will not stand by and see my daughter in such misery. Enough is enough! Isabella must be released from this engagement!"

"To repulse yet more suitors?"

"Mr. Chadbury, if our daughter has set her mind on remaining an old maid, then an old maid she will be. We meet the Tremaynes at the opera tonight. I beg you to speak to them. Think on't! Are you desperate to have a son-in-law who shrieks in Almack's—Almack's, mark you—at the sight of a mouse that strangely enough only he seemed able to see and then, recovered, tells bawdy lyrics to the gentleman? Is he of more value than Isabella's happiness?"

Mr. Chadbury looked at his wife in silence for a few moments. Then he said harshly, "Have you considered the social shame to yourself not to have secured a marriage for one of the most beautiful women London has ever seen?"

She made a dismissive move with one of her plump hands. "Pooh, what does it matter what they say? There will be no more Seasons for Isabella. We say we have spoiled her and yet apart from this one desire not to marry, she has proved a gentle and biddable daughter. We shall lose her love, and all because we tried to force her into marriage with a decadent popinjay. Would you have such a creature father your grandchildren?"

"Enough," said Mr. Chadbury wearily. "But say nothing to Isabella until we have had a chance to speak to the Tremaynes."

Lord Harry returned to his parents' town house in a black mood. The elderly retainer, Biddle, was sitting in the hallway playing with a cup and ball.

"Are you sober?" asked Lord Harry.

"I've done wi' drink," said Biddle gloomily. "It's what keeps us lower order from rising up against the likes of you."

"Yes, quite. How would you like a couple of gold sovereigns to fund the English revolution?"

"What have I got to do?"

"Find out what you can about a certain Lord Rupert Fitzjohn." Lord Harry handed him a piece of paper. "This is his address. Report back to me."

Biddle picked up an old-fashioned tricorne from the seat beside him and crammed it on his greasy locks. He was delighted at the prospect of some time out on the streets of London. Lazy and old the Tremayne servants might be, but nonetheless, Stokes, the butler, expected them to remain at their posts drunk or sober.

Biddle creaked his way through the streets of the West End. The day was still cold, and a thin fog made the lights of the taverns seem to beckon to him, but he went steadily on. He was fond of Lord Harry. He arrived outside Lord Rupert's house in Green Street and sat down on the front steps. As he expected, the door behind him soon opened and a butler came out. Biddle, twisting his head round, decided the fellow looked more of a thug than a butler.

"Move on, old man," growled the butler.

"I'm tired," whined Biddle.

The street was quiet, and Biddle's voice was unusually high and penetrating for such an old man. A window opposite popped open and a housemaid looked out, leaning her arms on the sill. She was a pretty girl with red hair and a jaunty cap.

"Get out of here or I'll throw you in the street," said the butler.

"Oh, you would, would yer?" screeched Biddle. "Here's me, an old sodjer what fought them bleeding Americans and got wounded in me back and you wouldn't even let me rest my bones."

"Shame!" shouted the pretty housemaid. "He ain't doing no harm."

The butler, by the name of Jakes, fancied the pretty housemaid, and so he pasted a smile on his unlovely face and said, "Here, step down to the servants' hall and I'll get you some ale."

With amazing alactrity, Biddle nipped down the

area steps and was shortly after admitted into the servants' hall.

One quick ferrety glance at the few servants who were seated at the table told Biddle that the master was probably a villain. There were two slatternly housemaids, one thin, indolent footman in grimy livery, and a small evil page. All were drinking ale. "Give this old pest some and send him on his way," growled Jakes before retreating back upstairs to see if he could engage the pretty housemaid opposite in conversation.

One of the housemaids drew a tankard of ale from a barrel in the corner and slapped it down in front of Biddle. "Whose livery is that, then?" asked the footman, eyeing Biddle's black velvet coat laced with silver.

"Got it out o' Monmouth Street," said Biddle, Monmouth Street being where the old clothes were sold. "Me in service? Nah. I wouldn't work for any of them parasites what battens on poor creatures like you."

"We don't do so bad," said the footman, tilting back his seat and swinging his legs up onto the table. He jerked his thumb at the ceiling. "His lordship is hardly ever home. Eats out the whole time."

"Decent sort, is he?"

The housemaids cackled with laughter, and the footman gave a sly grin. "He pays good wages so long as we keeps our mouths shut."

"You're making it up," said Biddle. "He's Lord Rupert Fitzjohn, ain't he? Can't hardly be on the thieving lay."

"No, but he lays everthink else," shrieked a housemaid and then threw her apron over her face.

"He ain't laid you, Marion," said the footman. "Not when there's all them Cyprians about. You should see some o' the parties here, old man. Make your eyes pop."

"Garn," sniffed Biddle. "I'm a traveled man. The things I saw in 'Merica. There's wimmin for ye." Biddle had never been out of England, but his dream had been to go to America, so much so that in his cups he often really thought he had been there.

"Ah, but them Yankees is puritans," jeered the footman. "Them and their Bibles. There's things goes on here you wouldn't see in them foreign parts."

"Such as?"

The footman leaned forward with a salacious leer and told Biddle about various parties and how at the end of one of them, Lord Rupert had taken three of the women to bed. "And they was lucky they got a bed," said the footman, nudging Biddle in the ribs so that some of the old man's ale splashed on the table. "Mostly he has them anywhere in the house, even the dining table."

"You set for another party tonight?" asked Biddle. "If so, you're mighty casual about it."

"Naw, he's going to the opera, and then he says he wants 'is curricle brought round at quarter to five in the morning."

"Why?"

"Race meeting, I s'pose. But he might have something else in mind. We've all been told to stay below stairs for the night and the whole of the following day." The footman winked. "And if we hears shrieks or suchlike, we're to stay deaf. So what does that tell you?"

"He's bringing some tart back."

"Heggzactly."

Feeling that he had found out enough and considering the ale poor stuff—Biddle did not consider drinking ale as *drinking*—he rose to his feet and made his way out into the London streets. But the taverns were somehow more welcoming than ever, and Biddle persuaded himself that he needed a reward for his efforts.

Lord Harry was preparing to go out to the opera when Biddle lurched in and fell on the hall floor. "What did you find out?" demanded Lord Harry, shaking the old man by the shoulder.

"He consorts wiff whores," slurred Biddle and closed his eyes.

"Leave him alone," said Captain James. "We'll be late."

"I suppose there is no use in trying to get sense out of him," remarked Lord Harry bitterly. "What a useless old fool. I should have known he would get drunk. No sovereigns for you, Biddle."

He turned away and drew on his gloves.

" 'Ere!" Biddle sat up in a panic that almost sobered him. "I earned it, so I did. He sleeps wiff half the Cyprians in London, that he does. Must ha' one coming round. Ordered 'is carriage for quarter to five in the morning. Told the servants to keep below stairs for the rest o' the day."

"Traveling carriage?" demanded Lord Harry.

"Naw, curricle. Where's me money?"

Lord Harry tossed down two sovereigns that Biddle fielded expertly, then he slowly collapsed back on the floor and was soon snoring.

"So what does all that mean?" demanded James.

"Something important, I think," replied Lord Harry. "I'll think about it some more at the opera. Where are my parents?"

"They're not going. Your father said he could not stand the caterwauling, and the countess agreed to keep him company."

Isabella could not help contrasting her own sorry state with that of Lucy's. Lucy, who had announced her engagement to the Chadburys, was happy and radiant, and the captain's eyes were glowing with pride and love as he looked down at her. Isabella could only be grateful that Lord Harry was quiet and thoughtful. She had expected him to start the evening in his usual way by making insulting remarks about her dress. The Chadburys were disappointed not to see the Tremaynes, Mrs. Chadbury in particular. She was anxious to have the matter settled before her husband changed his mind. She suggested in a whisper that they should tell Isabella *now*, but her husband said severely that they would call on the Tremaynes on the morrow, and she must be content until then.

"Two weeks until our wedding," said Lord Harry suddenly as he was leading Isabella into their box at the opera. She looked at him, startled, and then realized she had put the idea of the actual wedding so firmly from her mind that she had almost forgotten it was to take place so soon.

The opera was a new one by a Signor Belotti, and there did not seem to be anything about it to take Isabella's mind off her predicament. In the light of the huge blazing chandelier that hung down from the roof of the opera house, she could clearly see Lord Rupert in a box opposite. She looked straight at him and then slowly nodded her head. He smiled and raised his hand. Lord Harry noticed that exchange, and his eyes sharpened.

Isabella sat with her head bowed until the interval. She had done it. She had, by that simple nod, agreed to run away with Lord Rupert. Captain James, despite his own happiness, noticed how quiet and miserable Isabella was and experienced a feeling of impatience at Lord Harry's behavior.

At the interval when Isabella was talking to a friend of the Chadburys, James whispered to Lord Harry, "In faith, you are capable of driving that girl into anyone else's arms. If you are not behaving like a fop, you are behaving like a sullen pig, and so I tell you. Tell me, Harry, did you never *court* a woman?"

"I suppose I must have done." Lord Harry raised his thin eyebrows. "Why do you ask?"

"As you have not yet released Isabella from an engagement she so obviously loathes, then one must assume that you want her. So if you want her, try courting her."

"Tsch!" said Lord Harry moodily and wondered how it would feel to land a punch full on Lord Rupert's nose.

There was a ball after the opera. Lord Harry, waltzing with Isabella, found himself thinking of what James had said. Isabella's steps were not light. Her feet seemed to drag, and she made conversation in the way that she had been trained to do but barely seemed to hear his answers. He praised her gown and her looks, and she said in a dull voice, "Thank you. You are most kind," but he could have sworn she had not heard a word he had said.

His conscience was really hurting him now, and he tried to tell it savagely that his behavior had been justified. Isabella Chadbury was nothing more than a cold flirt. But there had been nothing of the flirt about her in London. He alone was to blame for her interest in Lord Rupert. And how happy she had been at the castle when she had run off across the grass with Lucy. There was one way to lighten her darkness, and that was by telling her that the engagement was at an end. But that would leave her free to marry Lord Rupert Fitzjohn, and that she must never do.

So while Lucy and her captain circled the floor and gazed into each other's eyes, Isabella and Lord Harry moved mechanically to the music and wished the ball would end.

It was Mrs. Chadbury who, thankfully for Isabella, said she must go home as she had the headache. Isabella promptly said she would accompany her.

Lucy was cross at having to leave so early but was soon consoled by Captain James, who said he would call for her on the following afternoon and take her driving.

Isabella gave Lord Harry a curt goodnight and

hurried off into the house before he even had time to bow to her and give her a formal farewell.

At his parents' house, he said good night to James and retired to his own room, but he did not go to bed. He paced up and down, turning over in his mind what Biddle had told him. Fitzjohn was a lecher. He had asked for his curricle to be ready at quarter to five in the morning. Isabella had nodded to him and he had acknowledged that nod, and he had smiled, a slow gratified smile.

Although they had left the ball early by society's standards, it was now three o'clock. He decided to stay awake and then walk to Malmbrooke Square to see if Lord Rupert made any move to take Isabella away. But surely he would in that case have asked for his traveling carriage. Nonetheless, Lord Harry was suddenly determined to go.

The minutes dragged, and he half dozed in an armchair in his bedroom until four o'clock. Then he roused himself and changed quickly into morning dress and wrapped himself in a warm cloak, after stowing a brace of pistols in his pockets.

Malmbrooke Square was not very far away. He set out on foot. He arrived in the square at four-thirty and stood in the blackness beside the railings of the square gardens, well away from the feeble rays of the parish lamps. At quarter to five, he heard the rumble of wheels and drew his hat down over his eyes so that the whiteness of his face would not show in the gloom.

Isabella had written a tearful letter to her parents, then had changed into a traveling gown and had packed a portmanteau and two hat boxes for the journey. She half wanted to wake Lucy to tell her what she was doing, but Lord Harry was Lucy's brother, and she felt that the girl's loyalties would lie with him.

She crept down the stairs. One of the hat boxes escaped her clutch and rolled to the foot of the stairs. It did not make very much noise, but to the overwrought Isabella, it sounded like thunder.

But it prompted her to speedy action. She ran down to the hall, retrieved the hat box, and holding it and the other securely in one hand by the ribbons and the portmanteau in the other, she stepped out into the black frosty morning. She saw the carriage at the corner of the square standing under a lamp. She placed her luggage on the step and turned and closed the door with a dreadful feeling of finality.

The curricle moved slowly round and came to a stop in front of her.

Isabella stepped forward and looked up at Lord Rupert. "Why a curricle?" she asked. "That will not take us very far north in this weather."

"They are repairing one of the traces on the harness of my traveling carriage," said Lord Rupert smoothly. "I will drive you to my house and you may have a glass of something to warm you while the servants bring the traveling carriage round."

Isabella hesitated, but then slowly climbed in and sat beside him.

The curricle moved off.

* * *

Lord Harry stepped out into the square and watched it go. She had gone willingly, without protest. There was nothing he could do.

"Ain't you going arter her?"

A voice behind him made him jump and turn round.

Biddle was standing peering up at him.

"What are you doing here, you old sot?"

"Saw you go out and came arter you," whined Biddle. "That was your lady went off with that pig."

"And willingly, too."

"Course she went willingly," jeered Biddle. "For that snake has tricked her some way."

Lord Harry stood irresolute.

"If it was me," said Biddle, "I'd go to 'is house and stand outside, like, see if she screams or summat."

The sheer idea of Isabella having to scream about anything galvanized Lord Harry into action. He set off at a run with Biddle stumbling after him, calling and protesting at the speed.

Lord Rupert helped Isabella down from the curricle and then sharply ordered a grinning groom to take the horses and carriage round to the mews.

"Come in, my dear," he said opening the door to his house. "A glass of wine to warm you."

"If I should be seen . . ." said Isabella nervously.

"It would not matter in any case as we are to be married. Just a few moments. We cannot stand here in this biting cold."

Isabella allowed him to usher her into the house. He led her into a library on the ground floor where a fire was burning brightly. The books on the wall had a uniform, unread look, which was indeed the case, Lord Rupert having ordered them by the yard from the bookseller.

She crossed to the fire and held out her hands to the blaze. There was a click from behind her, and she swung round. Lord Rupert grinned at her in a way she did not like and held up the door key before dropping it in his pocket. "That should stop anyone disturbing us," he said.

Isabella stood staring at him.

"Yes, my dearest, I am one of those disgusting men you so fear, who play interesting games with Cyprians on the floors of posting houses." He drew a pistol out of his pocket. "And now, Isabella Chadbury, you are going to learn everything a prostitute knows and better by the time I've finished with you."

White to the lips, Isabella said steadily, "Why?"

"Why, you bitch? Because you dared to spurn *me*, and no one insults a Fitzjohn without paying for it."

"Was it you who assaulted me in Cornwall?"

"Yes, and I would have had you in that ditch if that namby-pamby milksop hadn't come running up. Then you stuck a hatpin in me. Another thing you must pay for." He raised the gun. "Take your clothes off. The fire is nice and warm, and the hearthrug will serve us very well."

That was when Isabella began to scream.

"That's it," cried Biddle from outside the house. Lord Harry tried to run to the door but found the elderly retainer clutching his arm.

"Let me go, you old fool."

"I got the key."

"You've got what?"

"The key to the front door," said Biddle patiently. "I nicked it off the key rack on the way out from the servants' 'all, I did. Saw a spare and took it." He dug into his pocket and produced a large key with a label dangling from it marked "Front Door Spare."

Lord Harry seized it and went and opened the door and marched into the hall and stood listening with Biddle crouched behind him.

Inside the library, Lord Rupert was saying, "Scream all you like. No one will come to your aid. Now are you going to do as I ask, or am I going to have to shoot you?"

Isabella looked at him and said wearily, "Yes, you are going to have to shoot me."

He threw aside the pistol with a snarl and advanced on her. "Then I'll take you by force," he growled. "I'll rip those damned clothes from your body."

There came the sound of splintering wood as the library door crashed open. "Oh, I wouldn't do that if I were you," said a voice from the doorway. Isabella let out a moan of sheer relief as Lord Harry strolled into the room with a brace of pistols leveled at Lord Rupert.

"So it's you, you man milliner," jeered Lord Rupert. "How did you know she was here? Did the bitch tell you? Very brave with pistols, ain't you?"

Lord Harry grinned, and his blue eyes flashed, "I'll fight you, if you prefer . . . with my fists."

Lord Rupert threw back his head and laughed. "Splendid. We'll settle this here and now."

Both men pushed the furniture back helped by the eager Biddle. "No," said Isabella faintly. "You must not, Lord Harry. He will kill you."

Lord Harry did not hear her. Both men were engaged in stripping to the waist.

"Don't you worry, Miss Chadbury," said Biddle, settling himself comfortably in a chair in the corner of the room. He poured himself a glass of sherry. "Make yourself easy. Nothing better than a good mill."

Isabella sat down gingerly on the edge of a chair next to Biddle who handed her a glass of sherry assuring her it was a suitable drink for ladies, and he drank it himself when he was not drinking liquor, Biddle classing sherry with ale as innocuous.

"Strips well, don't he?" remarked Biddle conversationally, waving his glass in the direction of Lord Harry, whose well-muscled torso was gleaming in the firelight.

To Isabella it was all like some mad dream, the two half-naked men beginning to circle each other, the quite awful smell emanating from the old retainer. "Hey ho!" shouted Biddle. "Draw 'is cork, Harry."

And then Lord Harry leapt at Lord Rupert, raining savage blows on him, while the astounded Lord Rupert was sent reeling. "Goin' to be too easy," said Biddle, nudging Isabella in the ribs. "He'll finish him off any moment now."

Just as he spoke, Lord Harry landed a massive

blow right on Lord Rupert's chin, who stretched his length on the floor.

"Stop sitting there crowing, Biddle," said Lord Harry, "and tie this villain up. I want to have a long talk with him when he wakes up."

Biddle took out a wickedly sharp knife and began to hack the curtains into strips. Lord Harry dressed while Isabella sat there, wondering miserably whether *he* was about to take his revenge on her.

But when he was dressed he came and sat down next to her. "Tell me how you came to get yourself in such a dangerous situation," he said quietly.

In a flat voice, Isabella told him the whole thing, of the scene in the posting house, of her fear of men, of her dread of her forthcoming marriage, and of how Lord Rupert had tricked her.

"Why did you not tell me this before?" asked Lord Harry. "I thought you were a heartless flirt, and I only acted the part of the fop to enrage you."

"You succeeded very well." Isabella put her hand up to her brow. "So well that I could not confide in you."

"If only you had told me ..." Lord Harry took her hand in his. "As of this moment, you are a free woman. I will take you home. No one will be awake. You can simply go to bed and forget about the whole thing. No one will know. I will return here and make sure of that. Smile, Isabella. All your worries are over. I shall return to my regiment and you can forget this whole sorry episode. But there are plenty of kind and clean and decent men around who know how to love and respect a lady. Can you, for example, imagine my friend James consorting with whores? He loves Lucy truly, and she is prepared to follow him to the battle front. Such is love, something that men like this churl here know nothing about.

"Thank you," said Isabella brokenly. "Oh, thank you for everything."

He stood up and raised her to her feet.

"Like a play this is," said the irrepressible Biddle. "Kiss 'er."

"Impertinent dog. Watch your tongue."

"Well, don't 'e deserve a kiss?" whined Biddle.

Isabella kissed Lord Harry gently on the cheek, and he put his arms about her and held her close. They stood like that for a long time until they finally separated, looking at each other in a kind of wonder.

"Get a move on then," grumbled Biddle. "Can't stay here all morning!"

Chapter Nine

LORD HARRY AND Isabella walked through the still-
dark streets of London in the direction of Malmbrooke Square. All was quiet and still. Frost
glittered hard and white on the pavements, and the
parish oil lamps shone dimly through a thin veil of
fog.

"How did you know where to find me?" asked
Isabella. He was holding her arm, but it was comforting.

"I suspected Lord Rupert when I saw his horse
up for sale at Tats. He had sold it to a squire in
Exeter last June. I recognized that horse as the one
that had been ridden by your assailant."

"But why did you not warn me?" cried Isabella.

"Would you have listened? No. So I sent Biddle to
find out more about this Lord Rupert. Drunk as he
was when he returned—Biddle is usually drunk—he
managed to tell me that Lord Rupert had ordered his
carriage for five in the morning. It seemed to be nothing out of the way. He could have been starting off
early for some race meeting. But you nodded to him
at the opera, and I could not but help thinking it was
some sort of prearranged signal."

"He asked me to elope with him," said Isabella. She added timidly, "You did make yourself out to be such a monster."

"I can only apologize for having driven you to such lengths. You owe old Biddle a lot. I thought you were going with him willingly, but it was Biddle who pointed out that you had probably been tricked."

"He certainly deserves a handsome award," agreed Isabella. "But to get money to reward him, I would need to tell my parents everything. . . ."

"I shall reward him for you. But I doubt if there is anything the old man wants other than getting drunk from dawn to dusk."

"Could you bring him to me today so that I may thank him?" suggested Isabella.

"Certainly. I owe it to your parents to assure them that the end of our engagement is by mutual consent. I will ask to see you alone, and you may speak to Biddle then."

Tears stood out in Isabella's eyes. "I am so grateful to you," she whispered.

"Enough of that," he said harshly. "I do not deserve your thanks."

"You will soon be going away again, you and Captain James. Now that you are rich, why do you not sell out?"

"The war is unfinished. We must go on."

"And Lucy? She is so determined to go with her captain. I shall miss her sore."

They walked on in silence. Then Isabella exclaimed, "My luggage! I left it behind."

"I shall get it back to you without anyone knowing. Here we are. Enter quietly. Try to sleep and forget about the whole sorry affair."

He stood looking down at her, tall and serious.

"What will you do with Lord Rupert?"

"Persuade him to leave the country. I beg of you, forget him or that he ever existed." He raised her hand to his lips.

Isabella forget about the conventions, forgot that only a short time ago this was a man she loathed and despised. She threw her arms around him and hugged him close.

Then she released him and turned and fled indoors. He stood for a few moments, staring in wonder at the closed door, and then he went off to deal with Lord Rupert.

Lord Rupert, like most bullies, was a coward at heart. When Lord Harry said coldly he would kill him if he remained in England, Lord Rupert believed him. Lord Harry kept him tied up until he got a promise of a written agreement and then released him and waited until that agreement was written.

Then he took himself off to his parents' town house with Biddle following, carrying Isabella's luggage. "This be a bad business," moaned Biddle.

"Nonsense. It is all settled," said Lord Harry.

"I mean, here I am, an old poor frail creature, having to carry your lady's traps."

"Oh, give them here, you old reprobate. You are coming with me later today to call on Miss Chadbury so that means you are going to stay sober. I am going to lock you in your room."

Biddle let out a squawk of outrage. But Lord

173

Harry was determined, and so Biddle was thrust into the small cubby hole that served him as a bed-chamber as soon as they returned. Lord Harry turned the key firmly in the door and put it in his pocket.

He went to his own room and found James sitting there, waiting for him.

"I heard you go out," said James. "I looked at the time and remembered what Biddle had said about Fitzjohn. What happened?"

And so Lord Harry wearily sat down on the bed and told him everything. He did not think it necessary to swear him to secrecy, forgetting in his tiredness that James was too much in love with Lucy to keep anything back from her.

"I could call early," said the captain, "and take Isabella's bags with me. I could get them to her without being seen by her parents."

"What of the servants?"

"The Chadbury servants are too correct to make any remark. But just in case, I will wrap everything up in pretty paper and ribbons and they will think I have been buying presents for your sister."

Lord Harry yawned. "So all's well that ends well. Be a good chap and run along and let me sleep."

Captain James, carrying three huge beribboned parcels, which contained Isabella's two hat boxes and one portmanteau, presented himself at the Chadbury's town house. To his relief, he was told that Mr. and Mrs. Chadbury were still asleep but that his fiancée was in the drawing room. He made his way up the stairs, refusing to relinquish the parcels to a servant.

"Why, what is this?" cried Lucy, running forward to meet him.

"Not for you, my sweet," said the captain. "Here, shut the door and damn the conventions. I have such a tale to tell you!"

And so Lucy, sitting on his lap, was told the tale of Isabella between kisses. "Well, it is all Harry's fault," said Lucy when he had finished. "He could have made her love him."

"I sometimes wonder if he has any idea how to court a lady," said the captain. There was a noise from upstairs, and Lucy leapt from his lap. "My parents will be here shortly. I had better take these parcels to Isabella's room."

Isabella struggled awake as Lucy crashed in and dropped the parcels on the floor with a cry of, "I know *all*!"

"Does the whole of London know?"

"No," said Lucy, sitting on the end of the bed. "James told me all about it, but he will not talk of it to anyone other than me, and I won't tell anyone. Why did you not tell me you were afraid of men?"

"It was such a horrible experience, Lucy, not fit for your ears."

"Pooh," said Lucy. "You have led too sheltered a life, Isabella!"

"And you have not?"

"Well, no, for my parents are very lax, and I was allowed to run wild without a servant to accompany ... My dear Isabella, come the harvest festival, you have never seen such scenes of debauchery. I crept out to watch, but there was really nothing to it, rather like watching the beasts mating in the field, a lot more undignified but not alarming in the least."

"Oh, Lucy," Isabella was half laughing, half crying, "what a fool I am."

The Chadburys were preparing to go out to consult the Tremaynes about the end of the engagement when Lord Harry was announced.

They looked at each other in consternation. "It would be rude not to receive him. Perhaps we had better tell him what we are about," said Mr. Chadbury.

They received him in the drawing room. Lord Harry was accompanied by Biddle, a surly and furious Biddle, for he had been forcibly bathed and attired in clean linen. He felt a pale shadow of a man and kept swearing that they had washed all the strength out of him.

"Harry, my boy," said Mr. Chadbury awkwardly, "we are about to go to your parents. I am afraid Isabella does not want this marriage, and so we think it would be better if you cried off."

"Gladly," said Lord Harry with a smile. "But allow me some time with Isabella. At least I should be allowed to put her mind at rest as I have caused her so much distress."

Mrs. Chadbury heaved a sigh of relief. "Spoken like a gentleman. Of course you may see her. We will go to tell your parents the news."

The Chadburys waited until Isabella made her entrance. Mrs. Chadbury stared in amazement as

Isabella dimpled at Lord Harry and gave him her best curtsy. All her sympathy for her daughter fled. Isabella was flirting again.

When they had left, Lord Harry said with a glint of humor in his eyes, "Here is the horrible Biddle, who has done us such fine service. Biddle, the reason you are here is because we wish to show our gratitude to you."

"Gratitude!" shrieked Biddle. " 'Gratitude,' he says, and he gets me in the bath and washes me all over. Disgusting. You're spawn o' the devil, Harry!"

"Biddle!" exclaimed Isabella sharply. "Watch your tongue and do not address your master in that familiar manner."

"He can't help it," said Lord Harry amiably. "He was born a rebel. Well, you old reprobate. What is your reward to be? I suppose you want enough money to drink yourself to death."

Biddle sat down suddenly, and Isabella bit back an angry exclamation. The castle servants had been left to do much as they pleased for too long. No servant should dare to sit down in the presence of his betters.

"Anything?" asked Biddle, hugging his knees.

"Within reason, yes," said Lord Harry, half amused, half exasperated.

" 'Merica," said Biddle suddenly.

"America? Oh, not more of your maunderings, old man. I know you have never been out of England."

"Send me," said Biddle. "I want for to go to 'Merica."

"You're old and you might die before you ever saw it."

"Not if I had the best accommodation on board ship," said Biddle eagerly. His old eyes were shining.

"Why do you want to go to the colonies?" asked Isabella curiously.

"Because they ain't the colonies no more. Ain't no lords and ladies there. I can be free!"

"I' faith," drawled Lord Harry, "one would think we had kept you in chains. Very well, Biddle, America it is."

Biddle darted to the bell rope and gave it a hearty tug, and when the footman appeared, Biddle ordered champagne.

"There's no doing anything with you," sighed Lord Harry. "Go and have your champagne in the servants hall."

Biddle scuttled off.

"Good servant, that," said Lord Harry. "One of the best."

"But so impertinent and usually so evil smelling," remarked Isabella.

"He has a good heart, Isabella, and I would rather have that about me than a mincing posturing valet who knew how to shine my boots like glass."

"But you cannot just send someone so old off to the other side of the world just like that. He will need introductions."

"A cousin of ours has a plantation in Virginia. Biddle can retire there. So your parents know nothing of your adventures?"

"No, but Lucy does."

"Damn, James! I beg your pardon, but I did not expect him to tattle all over town."

"Only to Lucy," said Isabella. "He loves her, so naturally he told her. I would like to make one request."

"Your servant, ma'am!"

"I would like you to give me that quizzing glass of yours."

He unhitched it from around his neck and came and got down on one knee in front of her and held it up, his eyes laughing. "Here it is. Why do you want it?"

"I never want to see you stare at me through it again," said Isabella with a laugh.

"There are flecks of gold in your eyes when you laugh," he said softly. "Did you know that? And did you know your mouth becomes soft and tender and made for kissing? Do you remember our kiss, Isabella?"

She put a hand on his shoulder as he knelt before her. "Do not tease me, Harry. Do not mock me."

"I could no longer tease you or mock you if I tried." He dropped the quizzing glass to the floor and put both hands gently on either side of her face and kissed her softly on the mouth.

Fire seemed to course down from his lips through Isabella's body to her toes, bounce and soar up again, a fountain of fire and passion that burned against his mouth, melting all the years of ice.

At last he said huskily, "I should have done this from the first. Are you afraid of me?"

"No," she said. "No, not at all. Oh, Harry, we should not be doing this. I . . . I . . . mean it is not as if we are engaged any longer."

He swept her down onto the floor, gathered her

in his arms, and kissed her breathless. Then, holding her by both wrists, he stretched her arms above her head. "I am going to keep you here until you promise to marry me. Say, 'Yes, Harry.' "

"Yes, Harry."

"And I will take you to Spain with me, and everyone will be shocked and say, 'What a brute that man is to take the fair Isabella into death and danger,' but I will have you by me at night no matter where to have as I please until the day I die. By God, I love you!"

His kissed her so savagely that Isabella cried out and then kissed him back just as passionately.

Lucy, who had been sitting eagerly in the hall for Captain James to arrive, heard that cry just as her fiancé walked in the door.

"It must be Fitzjohn," cried the captain, rushing for the stairs with Lucy tumbling after him.

The couple stood transfixed in the drawing room doorway. Isabella Chadbury was rolling and groaning on the floor under the onslaught of Lord Harry's passion. Her once perfect gown was about her waist, and he was kissing her breasts.

Captain James gently drew Lucy away, a furiously blushing Lucy.

"Well!" exclaimed Lucy as the captain helped her into his carriage. "Whoever thought Isabella Chadbury could be so *naughty!*"

Mr. and Mrs. Chadbury were never to forget that day. Having secured the Tremaynes agreement to the termination of their daughter's engagement, they returned to find her sitting in the drawing room with a hurriedly *put together* look about her. Her hair was tousled, her mouth was bruised, and the tapes of her gown looked as if they had been quickly tied by an inexpert hand. Then the couple rose as they entered and dreamily announced they were going ahead with the marriage and that Isabella was to go to Spain.

Then there were all the sudden and hurried preparations for the wedding. Isabella, who had numbly gone through all the fittings for that wedding gown, suddenly deciding it wasn't nearly pretty enough and demanding changes.

The days flew past until the exhausted Chadburys found themselves at the double wedding, Lucy to her captain, and Lord Harry to their daughter.

Mr. Chadbury comforted his tearful wife as the couples drove off, heading for the wars. "I don't think we ever knew Isabella," sobbed Mrs. Chadbury. "It is a mercy she is safely married. So *wanton*. Every time I took my eyes off that couple, their hands were all over each other."

"Well, it's a happy wedding," remarked the countess. "Champagne is what you need, Sophia. Very soothing thing champagne!"

It was a relatively short war for Isabella. A year after her marriage, Napoleon abdicated and was sent to Elba to remain in exile. She and Lucy were thankful it was all over. They had not felt like heroines and had been frightened on many occasions and dirty and unwashed on many more. Now they were with their husbands in Paris, in a comfortable hotel, bathed and rested and dressed in clean clothes.

Lucy had gone out early riding with the captain, and Isabella was enjoying a late and leisurely breakfast with her husband. She was too thin, and her face was tanned and her dress simple, but she had all the easy manner of a woman who loves her husband and knows she is loved. Lord Harry looked at her affectionately over the top of his newspaper. He was glad she was safe. He often now wondered at his madness in taking her with him. The world was safe again, for that monster of a Corsican was on Elba and could not possibly escape. Isabella was reading a pile of letters that had caught up with them in Paris.

"What is the news?" asked Lord Harry.

"My parents are well, and everything seems much the same. I have a letter from your mother. She tells both of us that we must travel to Tregar Castle as soon as we can because it is changed beyond belief. She says they are very grand."

"Nothing about Biddle? He's probably dead."

"Let me see," murmured Lucy. "Perhaps there is something further on in the letter." She read in silence for a few moments, and then a look of surprise dawned on her face. "Why here it is. You will never believe this. Biddle is married! Your cousin wrote to your mother. Biddle is living in a cottage on your cousin's estate and has taken a wife."

"Some old crone, no doubt, some female Biddle," commented Lord Harry.

"Not a bit of it. He has married a widow of

thirty." Isabella blushed. "They are expecting a child!"

"Good for Biddle. He must be sober or he'd never have managed it." He threw aside the newspaper. "What would you like to do today, my love? Go for a drive in the Bois? Make calls?"

Isabella looked at him shyly. "I would really like to stay indoors with you. We have had little opportunity of late to . . ." She blushed again.

He stood up and walked round the table and drew her to her feet. Then he lifted her up in his arms and gave her a long, slow kiss. "My brave and gallant Isabella," he said, carrying her through to the bedroom and setting her down.

"I am not brave at all," said Isabella. "I was so very frightened, and one day when you did not return from the battlefield, I screamed and wept frantically and made a terrible scene."

"But you rode out to look for me all on your own!"

"That was because of Mrs. Malloy. You remember, the sergeant's wife. She came up to me and said, 'What are you screeching and caterwauling about. Faith, get out there and look for him.' "

He held her close, thinking he would never forget that day. He had been knocked unconscious when his horse had been shot from under him. He had recovered consciousness, lying among the dead under the blazing sun, dizzy and sick and faint.

At first he had thought he was dreaming when he had struggled upright and had seen the elegant figure of Isabella, picking her way through the bodies, leading her horse by the reins, her white muslin gown fluttering about her, and wearing a ridiculous straw hat crowned with flowers.

"But you came," he said, untying the tapes of her gown and letting it slide to the floor. "I am going to retire from the army now, and we will go home and raise a family."

"To Tregar Castle?" asked Isabella.

"No, my sweet. My mother's housekeeping would drive you mad. We will find a place of our own. Now about these children we are going to have . . ."